I0640098

IGNITION

William Hawk
EchoPress

MICHIGAN

Until the supernatural becomes more understandable to the natural world, there is no sense in trying to explain the reasons behind all the stories. There are truths buried in the words of this book, and it's up to you to discover and find the Proof of them.

I will, however, try to follow the example of selflessness that my mother displayed her entire life. She not only had eight children, but also fostered twenty-six more. Her love for others was unending. The most amazing thing about her was that she thought everybody was like that. Her zip code is no longer on planet earth, but her life continues to have a butterfly effect on countless individuals.

What a wonderful place earth would be if everyone echoed love like she did. In your mind, pick someone who you love and do one kind gesture a day in honor of that person. It doesn't matter if they're still here or have changed addresses. It will change you, and then that act will change those around you.

William. Come to me. Grace is here.

I can give her to you. I can give you all the girls you have wanted, all the things you do without. I can free you from your parents' chains. Everything—I can give you everything, William. Those around you are weak and pitiful creatures there to serve you.

Come to me.

CHAPTER ONE

I t happened very clearly on my sixteenth birthday. A switch was thrown inside my brain that gave me access to a world of memories I hadn't even known I possessed.

Before that day there had been a smattering of images floating in my memory banks that seemed quite vivid, yet foreign, as though they didn't belong to me. They had been crammed in there; stacked almost like an onion, layer upon layer, for as long as I could remember. I rarely could access more than the first layer, but I had always sensed there was more.

There was more, much more, and it was revealed to me on the morning of the first day of the one-hundred-and-ninety-second month of my life.

What had been mysterious became accessible, what had been indecipherable was decoded, revealing wisdom and knowledge that until that moment had been as far from my grasp as the edge of the universe.

But before that moment, it had been an ordinary day, as banal as any other. I remember waking up and hearing my brother, Cam, outside playing with our dog, Jett, and thinking, *Ugh, another day in paradise.* A boring weekend, then an even more boring week at school, no money, no car, still a slave to my parents, still an age where I was supposed to stay in line, get ready for college, shut up, and sit down. I craved adventure and excitement. Freedom. But I was sure that all I would really get was more of the same boring, blah-blah-blah life.

I slipped on a pair of graying shorts and a crumpled AC/DC T-shirt, a growing feeling of excess energy the only hint of extraordinary things to come. I splashed water on my face and brushed my teeth with the last blob left in a flattened toothpaste tube.

Heading downstairs, I tripped over a toy near the bottom of the steps. My mood morphed in the blink of an eye. I was a teenager. That's what happens. "Jett," I shouted to nobody, "why do you have to leave your bone at the bottom of the steps?"

My mother was in the kitchen. She called out matter-of-factly, "He's a dog, William."

Grumbling, I went to the refrigerator and yanked it open and stood there, staring at the ketchup and week-old Tupperware leftovers, in the way that we guys do when foraging for food. "What's for breakfast?"

"It's lunchtime," my mother said, "and I've made your favorite."

I glanced over. A small pot of tomato soup was bubbling, and a sandwich in the grill pan was browning, caramelizing in a lovely way. The scent of grilling cheese reached my nostrils.

"Look at the clock, honey," she said.

I did. It read 12:27 p.m. "So?"

"You were born exactly sixteen years ago this minute."

Oh, yeah. My birthday. I plopped down at the kitchen table.

My mother, a tiny woman with giant waves of curly brown hair that swished back and forth as she walked, hauled over the steaming bowl of soup and the grilled cheese sandwich.

"Happy birthday," she said. "Sixteen is a big year. My little boy is becoming a man. You will do great things for this family and the world."

She planted a kiss on the top of my head, but I couldn't feel it. Something strange was going on. Her voice faded and compressed, as though it were coming from some faraway place. I squeezed my eyes shut and shook my head.

Something weird was suddenly happening inside my skull. Was I going bonkers? Was I having a stroke? I fought back panic.

I peered around, feeling oddly changed. In the next nanosecond, my vision telescoped. My internal processor accelerated. I saw the kitchen, the house, the neighborhood, the world, and the universe, all bound together in a breathtaking, vibrating, color-saturated web. I grasped the table edge in a death grip with both hands and held tightly, my palms sweating against the wood. It felt as though gravity itself had amplified and was dragging me down in a series of cascading waves, each more powerful than the last. I was caught in the break zone of something vast and terrifying. I was horrified and exhilarated at the same time. What the heck was happening? Was it a brain tumor?

My mother had turned her back to me, cleaning up the kitchen. "Any big plans today?" she asked cheerily as my mind soared.

"Nope," I croaked, steadying myself, and then I staggered for the safety of my room.

I didn't know it, but my First Activation had just occurred.

In my room, I lay on my bed, catching my breath. I carefully positioned my head on my pillow and faced the ceiling. This was how Newton invented calculus, I remembered. He stared at his ceiling, studied the patterns in the wood, and built a new grammar of mathematics. Like me, he also thought he was going crazy.

I squeezed my eyes shut. The simple act of thinking had changed, and my enhanced awareness was struggling to adjust to linear time. Memories of things that had once been nothing more than whispers in my consciousness were now as vivid and as concrete as if they had just happened. In my mind's eye, I was seeing people I'd never known, and yet I somehow knew. They opened their mouths to speak to me...then dissolved into nothingness.

I realized I had to accept that something extraordinary was happening to me, though I wasn't sure what or how. Yet, somehow I *knew* that I didn't need a doctor or a shrink. I needed a plan.

The things that I had spent time thinking about before were now shuffled far back on my list of priorities. First, how was I going to navigate as part of my family without giving away the monumental change I'd just experienced? And what abilities did I really have? Was I now a superhero? Did I have extraordinary powers?

I wasn't sure. My gaze bounced from one object in my room to the next; it was as though I was unable to rest my eyes on one thing for too long. I blinked absently at the space posters above my bed. Then it hit me: What if I could move one of them with my mind? Telekinetically? It sounds crazy, but at that incredible moment, it seemed far from impossible.

I decided to try ripping a poster off the wall using nothing but mental powers. I propped myself up on my elbows and zeroed in on the poster, concentrating to the point of nearly giving myself a migraine. I couldn't get even the edge of the poster to roll up. Then I glanced over at my dresser, where an old fake Babe Ruth signed baseball sat on top. I squinted hard at it. *Roll, you stupid ball. Roll.* It didn't budge.

Last try. I plucked a penny off my nightstand and held it in my palm. I placed my other hand two inches above it. I concentrated with all my might, mentally trying to force the penny to leap. No matter how hard I tried, no matter what I imagined, the penny didn't even flutter.

I was not a superhero. I knew I was something different now, and I was sure the powers that I had just tried to control were in me, somewhere. Most importantly, I knew—*I knew*—that I had come into existence through a black hole.

And then the name Hunter came to me. I tensed.

Who the hell was *Hunter?*

Suddenly there was the fleeting image of a man who looked at me with cold eyes and had this wacked-out wink. As that image faded away another replaced it. It was a helmet. It floated in the air, spinning 360 degrees, and looked kind of like a hologram.

Then it was gone.

I jumped to my feet and paced my room like a feral animal. I couldn't shake it. The image of the helmet had imprinted itself in my mind—large, round, deep blue, with short twin antennae and a horizontal band of circuitry across the forehead.

And what was up with that creepy dude winking at me?

That was it. I couldn't let my thoughts go any further. I had to control this, keep it to myself, because if this wasn't enough to get me a free room with four padded walls, I didn't know what was. I walked over to my dresser and gazed at myself in the mirror. Here I was, still a kid, really, and out of the blue my life, my brain, my memories, my entire being had changed in an instant. But all around me, things were the same. Mom was in the kitchen. Dad was probably in the garage workshop, tinkering as usual. I wanted to tell them everything.

But no one would believe me.

I struggled to my feet, clutching my head. I would talk to my father, but in a roundabout way. He could help.

I stepped into the garage and found my father hunched over his worktable, a soldering iron in his hand. The blue flame reflected in the protective goggles on his eyes. His workshop was of the mad-scientist variety, kind of wacky and crowded with gadgets nobody but he understood.

"Hang on one minute," he said, scratching his bald melon. Seeing that made me wonder again if my hair would fall out someday. Lucky me.

I stood at the back of the room and looked around. This was my dad's den, his happy place, where he had the freedom to experiment with his endless wild ideas. He'd been trained as an electrical engineer and was proud to keep himself on the cutting edge. For a long time, he'd been working on improving battery storage, the great white whale of the field. I didn't know if he was still doing that anymore, because it was hard to get information out of him.

He turned off the soldering iron and lifted his goggles, blinking his bulgy blue eyes at me. "What is it, William?"

"I had a dream," I said, "and someone came to me and showed me a helmet."

"A helmet."

I nodded. "It was about this big." I spread my hands. "And it was blue, and there were two antennae, short ones."

I could tell my dad was trying not to smile. "Can you describe anything else about it?"

"There was circuitry along the top, right above the forehead."

"Hmm." He thought about that. "What do you think was this helmet's purpose?"

"I don't know, but I feel like I'm supposed to make it."

My dad finally broke out into a big smile. "And you want your old man's help?"

"Yeah. What could the thing be?"

He drummed his fingers against the workbench. "It came to you in a dream."

"Yeah, like it was a communication from someone in another universe or something."

"But it wasn't an astronaut's helmet."

"No," I said, "there was no faceplate. It was all open."

"But what does it do?"

I rubbed my forehead. "Maybe… it might help me think?"

"Think how?"

"I don't know. Get more out of my brain."

"Well, that couldn't hurt. They're developing technology now to read our thoughts."

"Maybe it's something paranormal."

My dad thought about that and grew pensive. "There's been some interesting progress in the world of ghost hunters. EVPs and such." He stroked his chin. "Is it okay if I sketch something out? Sometimes that helps me think."

"Sure."

"Stay here. This will just take five minutes."

My dad rummaged around until he finally produced a piece of drafting paper. Meanwhile, I roamed through the garage, looking at the debris, cut-up wires, discarded bits of cable, discarded motherboards, electrician's pliers.

I heard a sound behind me, and Jett trotted up to me with a drool-slicked toy bone in his mouth, the same bone I had tripped over. But as soon as we made eye contact, he stopped in his tracks. I watched as he began to tremble. Slowly, my faithful pet sank to the ground, as though someone were letting the air out of an inner tube.

I reached my hand down to pet him, and he let loose a strange yelp and slunk backward. I yanked my hand back.

My father looked up. "Quit hurting him, William."

"I'm not," I said.

"It sure sounds like you are."

The dog slunk off. But my dad didn't go back to his work with the drafting paper. Instead he stared at my hand.

"What's on your hand, son?"

I looked down. An X had formed on the back of my left hand. I felt my heart accelerate, my chest tighten. *What the hell?* I had no idea what it was, but I bucked up, tried to appear nonchalant.

"It's just something I drew in class," I lied. "Inside joke. Arthur drew one, too."

"Hope it comes off easy." My dad turned back to his desk. "Hey, why don't you give me a day or so to think about this?"

"All right. You don't think I'm crazy?"

He looked me in the eye. "Of course not, William. There's a lot about this world we don't understand yet."

I accepted that and turned around to leave the garage.

"And tell your mother that I want the roast beef for dinner."

"Okay."

I wandered back into the house and into the bathroom. I bent over the sink and splashed some icy water on my face and watched the beads slide down my cheeks.

This was really happening.

I slapped myself on the face. A red welt bloomed on my cheek.

I went to my room, grabbed my wallet and house keys, and headed out the door.

I had to go see Arthur.

✧✧✧

Arthur lived two blocks away. He was my best friend, and we'd known each other half our lives. He was a chunky guy with a meaty nose, beaming blue eyes, and too-long arms. He was mechanical too, like my father, and he liked working on cars. He was in the process of trying to fix up an old green Chevelle that an uncle had given him. He already had his driver's license and was really trying to get the thing functional. I was supposed to get my license soon, too, but had no ride of my own yet.

But now, suddenly, getting my license wasn't even on my radar.

Arthur was hosing off his car in the driveway. Without even a glance, he turned the hose on me. In half a second my shirt was soaked.

"You have got to be kidding me," I said.

"That's how we greet people around here on their birthday when it's eighty degrees out, Willie."

I should've expected something like that from Arthur. He could be such a practical joking pain in the rear.

"Don't call me Willie," I said.

"Sorry, Willie."

I stood there, just staring at him, trying to work up the courage to discuss what I'd been experiencing.

"You're acting weird," he said.

"I feel weird," I told Arthur. "It's not normal what happened to me today."

"Everybody turns sixteen, dude—it happened to me four months ago."

"No, something else happened. Promise you won't tell anybody?"

He continued hosing down his car. "Sure."

I sat down on the grass. "Have you ever thought about where we come from?"

He looked at me, puzzled. "You mean, like, from apes?"

"No." I struggled to find the words. "I don't know. Just…I've been thinking about how I maybe existed someplace else, before this life."

"You talking reincarnation?"

"Maybe. I don't know." I described everything to him, the visions, the telescoping reality, the guy and the helmet. The words came tumbling out of my mouth. I must have sounded strange because he shut the hose off and leaned against his car with his arms crossed.

"And this too," I said.

"What?"

I held out my left hand for him to see the strange cross. His eyes squinched. "William, you can't draw on yourself and say that some alien left his mark…"

"I didn't draw it, Arthur. It just appeared on me."

"Get outta here."

"Wash it off."

He turned the hose on the cross full blast. He held it there for a while.

"Damn," he said.

"You can't wash it off. I already tried. It's permanent."

Arthur's face grew darker, and he edged away a little. "I gotta be honest, man, you're freaking me out."

"I'm freaking *myself* out."

"But if you need any help, you know to call me."

"Thanks." I got to my feet.

"Hey, what are you doing with Julia today?"

I froze in my tracks. Julia. The girl I had a date with this afternoon.

"I don't know. I guess I forgot," I said.

Arthur was looking at me dumbfounded. "How could you *forget*? Everybody wants to hang out with that girl. I would cut off my arm for a shot at her."

"She's the last thing on my mind right now."

"If you need any help entertaining her, call me."

I grinned. "I'll let you know how it goes."

With that, I turned on a heel and headed back toward my house.

As much as I had wanted to be a sixteen-year-old and do the kinds of things that people my age liked to do, I was beginning to realize that was no longer possible. My mind was filled with an unbelievable mix of emotions, information, experiences, and memories that span lifetimes and centuries. At the moment, I couldn't make sense of the whole package. I needed to assemble this immense library that existed in my head into a pattern. Then I had to find a tangible course of action.

After I got home, I tried to text Julia, but my fingers felt like they were encased in cement. I didn't want her to be upset with me. As much as I wanted to get to know her better, it would just have to wait. *Sorry JJ don't think I can make it today, not feeling so hot.*

Almost instantly my cell rang. It was her. I'd expected as much. Julia was always very prompt in returning communication. I looked at the phone, listening to the ringtone, but I couldn't pick it up. She would know that I was avoiding her, since I'd just used the phone to text her.

Suddenly I felt my body erupt in lustful desire. Julia was a good girl who went to church every weekend, a pretty girl. I felt the memories of flesh, lips, breasts suddenly flood my entire nervous system. Then I realized something else.

Those weren't memories of Julia.

We hadn't done those sort of things. Those must have been memories from experiences that I'd had in some other time, some other place. But when, where?

Maybe another life? Then I wondered why I had even thought that. What the hell?

The phone went to voicemail and immediately began ringing again. I relented, took a breath, and picked up.

"Hey," I said.

"You're such a flake," she said. I could tell she was angry.

"It's just that something has come up," I said.

"What has come up, William? It's your birthday, and I wanted to see you."

Her voice sounded stressed. It occurred to me that she cared for me, a lot. She was the overly attached girlfriend.

"All right, fine," I said, without thinking. "Come pick me up and we'll go do something fun."

"What do you want to do?"

I spotted my muddy hiking shoes in the corner. "We'll go hiking at Bison Creek."

Silence from the other end of the phone. Then, "All right. Be ready by two o'clock."

Julia disconnected. I looked at the phone, thinking that I was disconnecting as well—maybe too much to ever be part of normal life again.

For the next hour, I pursued one of those harebrained ideas that make perfect sense at the time, but that seem totally ridiculous in retrospect.

I tried to burn off the mark on my hand. Well, first I scrubbed it with Lava soap, the stuff that is grainy and gets everything off. It didn't work.

Then I tried a steel bristle brush. That succeeded in ripping the skin off my hand, but not the mark.

Then I had one more idea. Fire.

Okay, I didn't say it was a good idea.

I found a magnifying glass on the basement "science shelf," as my dad called it. Then I went out to the driveway, where the sun was always the strongest on our property, crouched down, and held the lens about six inches above my hand. After looking around to make sure no one was watching this display of idiocy, I aimed that little point of concentrated sunlight in the center of the strange cross.

After a moment, it started to hurt. Then it *really* started to hurt. I gritted my teeth but kept my left hand planted against the concrete.

Across the street, a neighbor stepped out of her house. Her name was Miss Camille, and she was an eccentric. Nobody knew much about her, except that she liked to walk around and stare at people as if whatever they were doing was her business too. She was wearing a purple muumuu, like she always did.

She was staring at me. Though to be honest, I would've stared at me, too. The pinprick of heat had grown unbearable, and no doubt that pain was showing in my face. I swayed like a drunken sailor, dropped the magnifier, felt my body falling to the right, and I lost consciousness.

Then I had a vision.

Rolling green hillsides, yellow flowers lining the valley, the distant tinkling of a pristine silver stream.

I see a man fishing at water's edge.

"Where are we?" I ask him.

He slowly looks up at me, rubbing his beard thoughtfully. "We are here."

I realize conversation won't be ordinary with this man, and I rephrase the question. "Why am I here?"

He points toward the sky. "For the storm."

I turn my gaze to follow his finger. Above us the sky is a shade of blue a thousand times purer and more crystalline than I'd ever seen. "I don't see anything."

"It's always there," *he explains.* "See, a wise man knows when the storm is coming and finds a place to stay dry. Some people don't move in quite quick enough. They get sprinkled on, just a little bit. Others get a little wetter, but they're not soaked yet. So they take a little longer to dry off."

"And then?"

"And then there are those who get soaked to the bone. They don't seem to know when to come in out of the rain. And they may never dry off. Are you ready for the storm?"

I spin around, scanning the horizon. "But I still don't see anything."

He turns and looks me square in the eyes. "The storm is already here."

I came to. I was lying on my back on the driveway, the cracked magnifier next to me.

Above me was the inscrutable face of Miss Camille, wrinkly around the mouth and eyes, kind of rubbery, but not unpleasant. She dabbed the sweat off her cheeks with a handkerchief.

"You did it now, son," she said. "You passed right out."

I propped up on my elbows and looked at my hand. The cross was still there.

"There's something wrong with me," I said.

She looked at me with clinical detachment. "I'll say. What were you thinking, boy?"

"I'm not myself these days."

"Well, I used to be a nurse. Let me look at you."

She peered into my eyes, then put her fingers on my throat and found my pulse. Then she circled around, looking me over.

Finally, she circled back around. "Open your mouth," she said.

I obeyed. Miss Camille peered into my throat, cupped my chin, stuck her finger into my mouth, and tipped my head up. I felt like a horse that was being inspected for a sale.

"All your vitals look good," she said. Then she helped pull me up to my feet. I stood there, a little wobbly, my hand pulsing.

"Try to stop smoking pot, will you?" she said.

"I wasn't smoking pot."

"You don't have to lie. I come from a long line of hippies."

She winked at me. Then walked over to her house, turned back for another look at the village idiot, and shook her head before going inside.

At two o'clock, I heard a honk outside. I pushed aside the curtain. Julia sat behind the wheel of her Jeep, Ray-Bans up on her head. I grabbed my backpack and ran out the door.

I jumped in the Jeep and gave her a quick peck on the cheek. She seemed surprised. It was almost as if when I kissed her cheek I had given her a little electric shock. That would make sense, I thought, now that I had the First Activation engaged, though I was still foggy about exactly what this meant.

Settling into the seat, I turned on some tunes. I noticed her sketchbook at my feet. Julia was an excellent sketch artist, and I figured that she was going to work in a courtroom someday, drawing those charcoal sketches of the defendants.

"So where are we going?" she asked.

"The mall."

"I thought you said that you wanted to go hiking."

"I have to buy something at the mall first. It'll only take a minute."

As we pulled down the street, I drummed my fingers on the

door. The word *snaps* floated into my head. What were *snaps*? I became aware that Julia was saying something, but I couldn't really focus on what it was.

With effort, I turned my head. "Did you hear me?" she said.

"No," I said.

"Do you ever listen to anybody?"

"I've been distracted lately." It wasn't an apology, just an explanation.

"If you don't pay attention to me, I'll go out with one of the other guys who keep calling me."

That got my attention. "Like who?"

"Like Sean Wilder. And Thad Chadwick."

I felt jealousy shoot through me. It was a palpable pain.

"You don't want them," I said.

"How do you know that?"

It was time to play it cocky. "Because they are losers. And you like me more."

"You *are* different from other guys," she continued. "There's something about you that I just can't figure out. But you don't answer my phone calls, then you flake on me? It's, like, why am I with you?"

I didn't say anything to that, feeling that small wriggle of panic in my body again. I didn't want to lose Julia—that much was for sure. I would have to pay more attention to her once I learned more about what was happening to me.

We cruised for a few more minutes down the suburban boulevard to the local shopping mall. I'd been shopping here my whole life, and I knew the exact place that I had to go.

"Where should I park?" she asked.

I pointed to the right. "Over there, in front of the sporting goods store."

"What do you have to buy there?"

"Helmets."

She looked at me. "Are we, like, doing some dangerous hiking? Forget it, I'm not going dirt biking, no way…"

"It's not for us," I said. "It's for a project I have to do."

Julia parked, and we got out of the Jeep and headed into the sporting goods store. She followed me as I wound through the aisles, scanning for the helmets.

"Julia!" a voice said.

We looked over. It was some guy, the kind girls would probably call "handsome." He was taller than me, dressed like a golfer, and he had black hair and a big smile. He was everything I wasn't, and I hated him for it. I can admit that.

"Oh my gosh!" she said.

I watched my date, my girlfriend—I don't know what you want to call her—run over to this guy. I watched him envelop her in an embrace in his pumped-up arms. She pulled back. They spoke in low tones to one another. As if I wasn't even there.

I felt jealousy gathering inside of me. It surprised me to feel that, because I hadn't realized that I was so attached to her. Anyway, I wasn't the jealous type—they're real losers.

They continued talking. I could see the delight on Julia's face. I could see the smirking on his face as he made her laugh, and as she smacked him playfully on the shoulder. They were *flirting* with one another, right in front of me.

My whole body tensed. I felt the rage brimming within me. I looked down at the cross on my hand. It was glowing.

Then I sprang. But it was like I was outside myself, watching.

I sprinted over to him, hoisting him like he was a rag doll, and I threw him down the aisle. He went at least ten feet. I knew I was finding some of that special power I had envisioned earlier. His body crashed into a display of soccer balls, and they went bouncing all over the store.

"William," screamed Julia, "what are you doing?"

She tried to grab me, but I pushed her off. Still furious, I saw a rack of baseballs above his head. I held out my left hand, squinted at them, focused hard—and the rack tipped over. The baseballs rolled off the display and fell onto his back, one by one. He covered his head and shouted for help.

Julia gaped at me, seeming to be unsure if the balls had fallen at my beckoning or if they had simply toppled on their own. As I headed back toward the bozo she had been all over, she jumped in front of me, pushing me back.

Suddenly, I was as shocked as she was at what I had done. I tried to justify it.

"That guy was flirting with you!"

"That's Dean! He's my *cousin!*" she shouted.

I heard a gasp. To the left was a group of three women who were staring at me with horror.

"Did you see what he did?" one said, pointing at me. "He threw that boy like a wrestler!"

"Yeah," another said. "Then the baseballs nearly knocked the kid silly!"

The third said, "Wait, did this guy make the balls fall?"

The second: "Now, how in the world could he do that?"

"I don't know, but he was kind of pointing at them, then they…"

"Oh, stop it!" said the first.

"I'm calling security," said the second.

"Don't call security," said the third. "Call the *police.* That was assault!"

I stood there, breathing hard as the old gals' words drove the point home: I'd just assaulted Julia's cousin. In a rage of some kind that I didn't understand. With some ridiculous power that I'd never had before this morning.

Julia helped her cousin sit up. He wasn't hurt, but he sure was stunned at what had happened.

"Who *is* that lunatic?" he said. "Your boyfriend?"

They both turned to me with accusatory eyes. I saw a security guard appear near them. He looked at me.

"What's your name?" he said, starting toward me.

I stared at him, and then I turned and ran.

I sprinted as fast as I could, outside the store, across the parking lot toward the boulevard. I didn't know where to go. I had to hide, but this was totally new ground for me. Where did people go to escape the police?

I saw a bus slowing down at a stop nearby. The doors opened, and I sprinted across the grass and ran onto the vehicle. The driver sat behind a pane of glass with an angry look on his face.

"How much is it?" I said.

"You got a pass?"

"No. How much is it?"

He narrowed his eyes. "We only take bus passes."

I looked down at the meter. It had a slot to accept bills and another slot for coins.

"But this looks like it accepts cash," I pleaded.

"Naw, it's broken."

"Are you sure?" I said. I pulled a dollar bill from my pocket and held it at the front of the slot. The bus driver swore under his breath and leaned over and touched something under the machine. The small red light above the feeder slot turned on.

I fed my bill into the slot. It accepted it. I looked at the bus driver. He was staring straight ahead, impassive, a block of stone. "It was working all along. You just didn't want to turn it on."

"Please stand behind the line," he said.

"Do I get any change?"

"It doesn't give change."

"Where does this bus go?"

His eyes found me in the rearview mirror. "Where are you going?"

"I don't know."

"Then sit down, and I'll tell you when we get there."

He wasn't going to cooperate, not on anything. I walked to the middle of the bus, past all the others looking out the windows, and plopped down in a seat. A girl stepped on the bus and came and sat a few rows behind me. I kept thinking that she was looking at me, but every time I turned for a peek over my shoulder, her face was turned away, against her shoulder like she was napping.

"William," I heard her say, but again, she wasn't looking at me. I was hearing things. Maybe I had gone over the edge.

The bus pulled away from the curb.

We drove about a mile and stopped, letting people off. Then we drove another mile and did the same. A couple people got on; even more stepped off. After driving for about thirty minutes, we'd left the city behind and were now out on a lonely two-lane road, desert all around. There were only three of us on the bus now: the driver, the girl who got on the bus at the same time I did, and me.

The driver's eyes found me in the rearview mirror and looked at me as though he could see into my soul. "Last stop," he said.

I peered at the barren landscape around me. "Where exactly are we?"

The bus driver shrugged. "I don't know the name, but it's a few miles from the middle of nowhere. That's for sure."

"That's fine by me," I said.

The bus slowed to a stop. As I walked past the man, he caught me by the arm. His grip was strong, and it took my breath away. I turned my face to his. The man's eyes were full of pain. "You be careful out there."

"I will," I said. "There's still one more girl on the bus."

He looked in the rearview. "I don't see anybody."

He was right; the bus was empty. I hadn't seen the girl leave. Somehow, I knew she was still there, but I shrugged, stepped off the bus, and heard the doors close behind me. I watched it pull away and disappear into the distance.

I was alone.

CHAPTER TWO

The aging security guard helped Julia take her cousin Dean to the back room. She couldn't believe what had happened.

The store manager, with his flattop haircut and a nose like a potato, hovered over them, concerned. "We reviewed the security footage," said the manager. "Kind of funny how that nut job pointed at them baseballs and then they whacked you on the noggin."

Everyone was silent for a moment, and all Julia heard was her heart thumping in her chest.

The store manager cleared his throat. "Coincidence, I guess. Unless you believe in witches, which I don't."

Dean blinked at them. "I don't even remember what happened."

A worker dressed in a black-and-white referee's outfit, the uniform of the store, came in through the swinging door.

"So, the county sheriff is here, and he wants to see Julia."

She buried her face in her hands, not wanting to face him. "It's my dad," she told them.

"Your dad is the sheriff?" asked the manager.

"Yes."

"Well, shit."

A minute later, Julia's father strode into the room. He wore the full cop getup that she had seen him leave the house in every morning since she could remember. He wasn't the type of man you messed around with; she had seen some men try and pay dearly for it.

"Sheriff Winters," he said, introducing himself to the manager. He turned and saw his daughter. "Julia, you okay?"

He put his hand on his daughter's shoulder.

"I'm fine. It's Dean here who got tossed around."

Sheriff Winters turned to his nephew. "What the hell happened?"

Dean looked up. "That boyfriend of hers attacked me. He's psycho."

The sheriff turned to the manager. "Do you have the tape?"

Not the tape, Julia thought. She was mad at William, but still wanting to protect him from the likes of her father. *And the baseballs—what the hell was that about?*

They went back into the store, toward the security room. Through the swinging door, Julia caught a glimpse of a very odd guy about her own age, arrogant looking, standing in the aisle straight up like a Marine. Brown hair, smooth skin, and cold, empty eyes. He was dressed in a navy-blue pinstripe suit with polished dress shoes—not the usual outfit of her age group.

And he was looking at her with those shark eyes.

A chill went down her spine. What was it about this guy?

Her father pushed past her. "We're gonna take care of this. Come on, kids. I'll give both of you a ride home in the squad car."

She hurried after her father, tapping him on the shoulder. "Dad, look at that weird kid back there."

The Sheriff turned. "Back where?"

Julia hesitated to look at the oddball again, but she mustered her guts and turned around. "Right over…" she said, but navy-blue suit was gone.

She and Dean followed her father back into the store. The sheriff said, "Julia, what was William's last name again?"

"Hawk."

"William Hawk," he said to himself, "you are in for a world of hurt."

As they went out the front door, Julia knew that the weird boy had left, but somehow, she still felt his chilling gaze on the back of her neck.

CHAPTER THREE

For the next half-hour, I stood in the fields, watching the occasional car whiz past me, not sure what to do. An experienced hobo could've told me the best routes to take, which ones to avoid, how to eat, how to skulk. I was going to have to teach myself all those skills.

Welcome to life on the run.

I walked along the shoulder of the road, feeling the pebbles of the gravel skittering beneath my shoes. The sun was sinking toward the horizon. I had to figure something out, and soon.

The first thing I admitted was that I didn't know myself anymore, didn't know what I was capable of, and so should take sufficient care to keep myself calm. I'd totally misjudged the situation in the sporting goods store and had nearly bludgeoned Julia's cousin with a telekinetically tipped rack of baseballs. Who knew what else I could do?

Then I thought about the legal ramifications.

They'd certainly called the police. Which meant I would be in trouble if I went home. I knew I had to soon, but I was going to put it off as long as I could today.

That wrecked me. This day was turning out so very different from how it had begun. I realized I had wanted the day to be different. What if I was getting my wish? Could I un-wish it now? Boring sounded pretty good at this point.

I struggled along the road, gusted by the blast of wind with every passing car, preoccupied by my dilemma. There seemed to be nowhere to go.

At last, with the sun touching the horizon, I felt fear plucking the strings of inner panic and decided to try hitching a ride. It didn't matter to where, as long as it got me farther away from my town.

I heard a car approaching. I turned and stuck up my thumb. It roared past me, my hair flying in the wind. In the next hour three more cars did the same.

The problem was that I was a teenage boy, alone. Nobody in their right mind picks up teenage boys. It would've been easier if I'd put on a wig and a miniskirt, but I didn't have the legs for it.

Night had fallen, and all around the locusts were chirruping in the fields. I was tired, dehydrated, and absolutely panicking at the prospect of sleeping in a corn patch, but I had no choice now. Cars had been rare, and now I saw none. So I made my way into the pitiful desert cornfield, and I tore off stalks and leaves and made myself a bed—it reminded me of the ones I had seen chimps make on a *National Geographic* show. I lay down and covered myself as best I could, thinking I'd be up all night, but, exhausted, I soon crashed.

I awoke to sunlight and bugs and corn all around. I felt as still as one of those cobs. Grunting, I got to my feet. I must have slept quite a while, because the sun was already almost directly overhead.

Back on the highway, my stomach growling and my mouth dry as chalk, I waited. And waited. Then a big black Mercedes came blowing by me, not even slowing down as I stuck out a thumb. More cars whizzed past. Then I spotted a vehicle humming down the road my way. I couldn't make it out at first, then finally I could see that it was an old truck. And it was slowing down as I stuck my thumb out.

As it drew closer, I saw that the vehicle was a rickety pickup truck older than I was. Just a few streaks of green paint were still visible through the rust. Its springs squeaked rhythmically as it shuddered to a stop in front of me.

I let the driver get a good look at me, then hustled over to the passenger door and leaned in.

The driver asked, "Where are you going?" The driver was a man, but I couldn't get a good look at him yet.

"Away from the city."

"Then get in."

I hopped inside the cab and shut the door. The driver put the truck in gear and pulled back onto the road. As soon as I felt comfortable, I took a look at the driver. He was an older man, maybe sixty-ish—it was hard to tell—with shoulder-length, salt-and-pepper hair. He wore a beaded leather vest and intricate turquoise jewelry, suggesting that he lived on the nearby reservation. He had a leather-tanned face, with broad cheekbones, silver eyebrows, and an inscrutable expression.

He peered at me under those silver brows, his eyes ancient and his gaze intense and intimidating. "What's your name?" he said softly.

"William," I said. "Yours?"

He paused for quite some time and did not even blink,

just stared at me out of the corner of his eye. I wondered how long it would take for him to respond.

"Before I tell you my name, I must first tell you a story."

"Okay," I said, with a shrug. I was in no position to insist.

He drew a deep breath. "I've never seen a seeker, but the Ancient One said that you will know one when you see one."

"Okay," I said again. That sounded strange but interesting. Surely this stranger couldn't have any idea what was going on inside my head. I waited. What else could I do?

"All things are connected, fed by the energy in the sky. Some of the energy is a good stream, and some is a bad stream. Each of us has a reservoir around ourselves that needs to be filled by these streams. We can choose which one to fill us. I can see your reservoir."

"You can, huh?"

"Most people have it maybe this thick." He held up his thumb and forefinger, about an inch apart. "But yours, yours cannot be contained inside of this vehicle. You have so much to fill and so much to give. The only question is—which stream will you use to fill it up?"

I didn't know what to say to that. Who was this guy? Was he just an oddball, someone who gave this New Age rap to every hitchhiker he picked up? Before hacking them to death with a chain saw? I looked in the back of the pickup. No chainsaw.

"Now tell me what you're running from," he said.

"Life," I said.

"I see. So where do you think you might be headed?"

"I have no idea."

The old man settled back in his seat. I got the odd feeling he knew everything that was happening was predestined. "I have a cabin out on the reservation. Do you want to go there?"

"Am I allowed?"

"Why wouldn't you be?"

"I'm not native. I heard that there were places there that only natives were allowed to enter."

"Maybe, but anybody can enter the reservation."

"In that case, it sounds fine to me."

That answer seemed to satisfy him, and we didn't say much more for the next few hours. I felt the truck sway and rumble as he nimbly navigated the turns in the road that led up into the high-altitude forest.

It was late afternoon when the truck pulled up to a small cabin tucked on the edge of a wooded valley. The structure had been simply built, just stacks of logs with corner notches.

The old man got out of the pickup with much effort and gestured to the house. "Many generations of my family have called this home. Behind the cabin is a steep canyon, so don't wander too far to take a piss at night or you'll break every bone in your body."

I still hoped this guy wasn't dangerous. I followed him into the cabin. It was a comfortable room with an old bearskin rug and a bed in one corner and an old sofa in the other. I sat on the sofa and watched the old man toss a couple chunks of wood on the fire.

"You never told me your name," I said.

He drew a deep breath, and his face puffed up as if he were in physical pain. At last he said, "People usually call me Cy."

That sounded as though it was short for something. "Does it mean anything?"

"Sure does," he replied. "It's short for *sight*. You see, there's a lot more in this world than what most people see, but you can only see it if you have special sight. Just like me seeing you, I knew you was different. You're a seeker. You and me got a lot to teach each other. You see, people have just about lost touch with who they really are. We've let our spirit become so dormant in us we hardly know how to connect with it anymore. And you—I've been told about you."

Told about me? I looked at the old Native American, wondering if he too had seen life the same way that I'd seen it a day ago. All signs indicated that he had. I hoped so. I didn't want to be the only one.

He asked if I was hungry. Was I ever!

We had sandwiches and drank some kind of juice concoction that he said put hair on your gonads. Mostly we just rested up as night came on.

Then Cy pointed to a single mattress in the corner with some old Navajo blankets thrown on top. "You can sleep there. Stay as long as you need."

I staggered over and collapsed on the mattress, totally exhausted from the events of the past two days. Cy set down a glass of water on the floor next to me, and I drank the whole thing in one swallow.

Then I lay back down again, watching the tongues of fire lick the inside of the chimney, feeling hypnotized, like the best fires always make you feel. I let my thoughts wander. They flitted around between the family, friends and possible lawsuits that I was leaving behind. Then sleep overtook me, and I had strange dreams unlike any I'd experienced before, where people seemed to be trying to tell me something, though their faces and voices were blurred, and their messages garbled.

The next day, I sat with my pants around my ankles, trying to remember those foggy dreams.

I was in the privy that Cy had built adjacent to his cabin. This was the only place you could do your private business. It was ironic, I thought, after my ethereal experience last night, to be here in such a primitive way.

When I got back to the cabin, I saw Cy coming out of the woods. He had a bag slung across his back.

"Do you want some breakfast, William?"

"Yes, sir," I said.

We entered the cabin together. He set some water boiling, and a few minutes later, I was digging into a bowl of instant oatmeal. I could feel him watching me.

I looked up at him. "Aren't you going to eat anything?"

"No, I already had some breakfast."

"What time is it?" I asked between bites.

"Almost eleven o'clock," he said. I could feel him studying me. "Something happened to you recently. Something staggering."

"How do you know that?"

"I can feel it."

I swallowed and put down my spoon. "I have had a strange time of it the last day or so."

Cy nodded and listened as I told him the strange experiences of the last two days. He didn't seem the least bit surprised. After I'd finished, he spoke. "My forefathers have passed down stories from generation to generation. They spoke of the great ones that had achieved harmony. Not harmony with self but with every living thing. My people have tried and tried for millennia to achieve this. There have even been stories told of whole civilizations perishing, then reigniting. I don't know if these stories are based in fact. But I do know that the more one focuses on self, the less they can see it."

At that moment, I knew for sure that I could learn a lot from Cy.

The rest of the afternoon, I made myself comfortable at Cy's cabin. It was a spartan space with rough-hewn wooden furniture and a primitive sink. A few native throw blankets with geometric patterns were the only nods to comfort. I didn't quite understand why he lived such a meager existence, since there were plenty of geological treasures on the shelves, on the chairs, on the floor. By that, I mean gemstones and raw minerals. Chunks of gold embedded in rocks the size of basketballs. Uncut raw diamonds the size of peach pits in a mason jar.

"Cy, why don't you sell some of this stuff? You could live a better life."

He was sitting in his deerskin chair, looking gaunt. "They're not mine to sell."

"If you found it, then you can sell it."

He looked at me as though from a great distance. "Nobody owns the earth. We're just caretakers."

He left it at that, and I didn't try to ask him what he meant.

The second morning, I woke up to an empty cabin. I lay on the humble mattress, smelling the odor that was rising from beneath my arms. I hadn't showered in a few days, and it was becoming noticeable.

I stumbled over to the kitchen and made another bowl of oatmeal and ate it in silence. This was how life was going to proceed for the moment—weird, yet somehow still ordinary.

I went out onto the porch of the cabin, pulled on my shoes, and began to explore the property. Cy hadn't done much to his little homestead. It was just trees, bushes, a few glens where there must have been underground water, and the valley, which opened wide off to the side. A small vegetable garden had been dug into the hard, rocky soil, but that was about it for landscaping.

I went and stood at the edge of a small cliff near where the land dropped away into the valley. On the far side of the valley was another house. It wasn't too far as the crow flies—I could even make out a figure sitting on the porch. But to navigate down into and up out of the valley would take quite a while.

I thought about going over to explore, but then I thought better of it. I turned and walked back to the cabin and sat down on Cy's favorite deerskin chair and thought about my circumstances.

An hour later, Cy returned from wherever he had gone. He saw me sitting in the chair. "You know what the source of all of mankind's problems is?"

"What?"

"We can't do what you're doing. Sit in a room and be content. You've got the solution to all of life's problems."

I gave him a half-smile. I certainly didn't feel like I had the solution to anything at the moment.

"Where did you go?"

"Out," he said, not looking at me.

"Same place as yesterday?"

"Why are you so curious about what I do?" he said, "Why don't you tell me what *you've* been doing?"

I shrugged. "I walked around the property. I saw your neighbor sitting out on his porch, on the other side of the valley."

"That's Sonny. He's been living here since the beginning of time it feels like. I was going to head over there this afternoon. He's got my shovel that I need to get back. You want to come?"

That surprised me. "You want people to know that I'm here?"

"I trust Sonny," he said, "and I'm sure that Sonny would want to meet you."

❖❖❖

An hour later, we were going through the trees, down into the gulch, and then scrambling up the side of the hill. The soil got under my fingernails, and the knees of my pants were caked in dirt.

"Isn't there any easier way to get there?" I said, out of breath.

"We could drive," Cy said, "but the road is around the other side there, and it takes forty minutes. This is the way I've always preferred. Closer to the earth."

When we reached Sonny's house, I saw the figure that had been on the porch. This time, he was in his driveway with a brush in one hand and a can of stain in the other. He was slathering the stuff all over a decrepit rocking chair. As we drew closer, I saw that Sonny was an extremely old man. Behind him, his ramshackle cabin looked shabby but decently maintained. He was the type of old man who could keep up around the house.

"Sonny," said Cy, "I come for that garden shovel. And I brought somebody you'll want to meet."

The old man turned and looked me up and down with eyes as dark as coal. I did the same to him as he turned and walked toward me, his movements fluid for such an old dude, his body slim, wiry, kind of taut, like he had been a professional boxer back in the day.

"Pleasure," he said.

He offered his hand and I reached out and shook it. A surge of energy passed between us. It was so strong that I fell backward and shook my hand out. He didn't seem perturbed.

"I saw you sitting on your porch this morning," I said.

Sonny had gone back to staining his chair and didn't say anything. I could tell that he was the stoic type. It looked like it was physically painful for him to form words.

"Sonny is a porch sitter," said Cy. "Early morning and late evening, sunrise and sunset, he's there. Watching out for us."

That sounded puzzling to me. "What are you watching for?"

The two old men glanced at one another. Cy spoke first. "There is a lot you don't know, William."

"Danger," Sonny said.

Cy went over to a small shack and threw open the door and busied himself with rooting around inside. I could see a vise, several calipers, power saws, and other tools of a workshop. I guessed that self-reliance was necessary when you lived as independently as he and Cy did. You had to know how to fix things, and he did.

Meanwhile, Sonny said, "How long have you been here?"

"A few days. I don't know how long I'll stay."

"This valley has some special sites." He nodded for me to follow him. We walked to a small promontory a little ways away. He still carried the paintbrush.

He pointed to the valley bottom, to an open spread of land that was about a quarter mile north of where we'd crossed. "There," he said, "is the cemetery where our ancestors are buried."

"Cy didn't tell me about that," I said.

"It's closed to outsiders. You can't get in."

I smirked. "I sincerely doubt that."

He ignored me. "And up over there is a…"

I waited for him to finish, but he never did. "Is what?"

"Something that we've long forgotten about. Our people have some legends." He paused. "It's better just to leave that one alone."

He turned away from me and went back to his chair. By now, Cy had found his shovel and was waving for me to return.

"There's a cemetery down here?" I asked as we descended into the valley.

"Yes," he said.

"Are you going to take me there?"

"No, they won't let you in."

"Who? The staff?"

He looked at me oddly. "No. Let's keep moving."

He gestured for me to go in front of him, and as we crossed the valley on the way back to his cabin, I got the sense there was a lot that Cy wasn't telling me.

My third morning in the cabin, I woke up to the sound of the door closing. The sun was just starting to peek through the windows.

Groggy, I went over to the door and saw Cy disappearing down a path into the trees, a bag slung across his shoulder. Curiosity called me. I pulled on my pants and shoes and, without even so much as a drink of water, crept out of the cabin and followed him down the path.

It wasn't an easy hike. The route wound up a steep path that was paved in asphalt, then turned into a wide fire road, then narrowed to a small path again that hugged the side of the cliff. I stayed far enough behind Cy that he couldn't see me.

Then he disappeared around a hairpin curve. When I arrived there, the trail ahead was empty. He hadn't started running, that much was certain, so he must've gone off the path.

I scanned the dry forest slope beneath me, looking for a sign of movement.

There.

Down the slope, and a considerable way to the south, was a small plateau of rock. A figure quickly crossed it and swung down and out of sight on the other side.

Cy.

I plunged into the forest and began running through the trees, smelling the pine, feeling the needles crunch beneath my shoes. The shadows dappled on my forearms.

At last I arrived at the small plateau. I ran to the edge and looked down. There was a rope tied to an eyebolt that had been drilled and fastened into the rock. The rope disappeared over another lip of rock a little farther down.

I had to follow.

I waited a couple of minutes, so that Cy wouldn't see me if I happened to catch up. Then I picked up the rope and tugged on it. It felt secure. I gripped it with all my might and began walking backward down the face of the cliff.

Four steps, and I hit the lip. I paused and looked down over my shoulder. The floor of the valley was about thirty feet below me. I could handle this. I let out the rope, took a breath, and continued walking backward down the wall. My biceps strained with every release and catch.

I was a few feet from the ground when the heel of my shoe caught on a small outcropping. My body pinwheeled and I found myself falling headfirst, the rope burning my palms. I managed to twist around. My body bounced on the rocky valley floor. I moaned in pain and lay there for a while.

Eventually I sat up and looked around. The valley floor was hard here, with rocky soil and piles of schist bulging up out of the ground like unknown growths from the ancient center of the earth.

Then I saw it.

A cave.

It was a decent-size opening, maybe ten feet tall and wide, and it stretched away from the daylight into darkness. I knew immediately that this was where Cy had gone.

I pulled myself to my feet and entered the cave, allowing my eyes to adjust to the dark. You wouldn't think that dirt smelled like anything, but this cave did, like dirt and rocks and the million years that it had been there.

"You're quite the adventurer," said a voice.

I whirled around. Behind me stood Cy, the bag slung around his back. His eyes seemed alive, and his jaw was working on something that looked like gum.

"I'm just curious," I said, lowering my head. "I heard you leave yesterday morning too, and I just wanted to know where you were going."

He approached me and grabbed me by both shoulders. I kept my face down from shame. "Look at me, William," he said. I lifted my face and looked at Cy. He was only a couple inches shorter than me, but he was making me nervous. He had an enormous presence that demanded respect.

"You need to make a decision," he said.

"What kind of decision?"

"Whether you want to enter this cave and learn, or go back home."

My eyes searched his. "I think I want to learn."

His lips scrunched up, as though my response caused him great consternation. "That's the more difficult path." He thought for a moment, and then pushed a finger against my sternum. "It's clear that you have some kind of power. I've already told you that."

I felt my heart hammering against my chest. "I don't know what's happening to me."

"How old are you?"

"I just turned sixteen."

A smile curled the edge of his lips. "It's your decision."

I made my decision. I nodded.

He stepped into the darkness that stretched out behind us. "Follow me."

CHAPTER FOUR

The High School

As Troy leaned against a wall in the hallway, waiting for his girlfriend, and lunch, a freak in a navy-blue pinstripe suit walked stiffly into the high school and looked around as though it had never seen one before.

The freak in the suit stood just behind the door, away from the hustle and bustle of the hallways—girls laughing, boys roughhousing, backpacks aplenty, all streaking by him.

His face seemed to just take it all in.

Troy said to no one, "What's his deal?"

Troy didn't like suits, didn't like freaks. Didn't like the school or his girlfriend much, either. People were pains in the ass, and he was the painkiller.

"Hey, freak boy!" he shouted over to the suit freak, but then another guy jostled the freak, told him to watch it. The face above the navy-blue pinstripe suit just looked at the student as though it were an insect. The nose twitched.

"Which way is the office?" Its voice came out clean and high and strange.

The student paused. It seemed to Troy that the suit freak was a wimp, backing down suddenly. "Down there, on the right."

Troy had to see what the deal was with this guy, so he followed the freak.

The navy-blue suit moved down the hall, unbothered by the commotion. Boys and girls gave it a wide berth, a few making snide comments about the suit.

One aggressive kid wearing a pair of earbuds came up to the freak. "Hey, this ain't the bank. What you think, you gonna hold all my money? I ain't givin' you a deposit or *nothin'*."

The suit stared at him, and the mouth began to speak. "I am not a student."

Yeah, thought Troy. At least this dude is gonna kick some ass.

But strangely, the earbud guy stepped back. The suit freak proceeded down the hall to the office, and Troy fell in close behind. As the suit stepped inside, his freaky expression changed, suddenly becoming friendly and smiling.

The registrar behind the counter—someone Troy knew to be a complete loser—glanced up.

"Yes, what is it?"

"I'm looking for a William Hawk," said the freak. The voice was now professional, but as friendly as his grin.

She snapped, "So are we. Who are you?"

"I'm his cousin."

Yeah right, thought Troy. *Even this stupid woman should know that's a load.*

"I wish I could help you."

Troy thought, *No, you don't.*

"What's his address?"

"You're his cousin. Why are you asking me?"

The smile on the face grew tighter. "I lost it, and I've never been to the family's house." Then, like he just made it up: "We always meet up north on the lake in the summers."

"Can't help you."

The freak leaned in, real close. "But I need it. Now."

And suddenly, like the other clueless idiots around there, the woman seemed to back off. *What the hell?*

"Why not?" she said, not taking her eyes off the suit. "Your name?"

Troy had a good angle on the freak's face now, and he could see the guy reading the little sign on the wall behind the registrar's head.

The sign said, "Lord, grant me patience... but do it now!"

"Patience."

"Patience?"

"Yes. John Patience."

Troy laughed, and the freak gave him a look. For a second, Troy thought maybe this *was* one bad dude, maybe the others knew something, but then he straightened up and shot back an intimidating look himself. No freak in a monkey suit was going to scare him.

After the woman jotted down his name, she clicked through the school directory on the screen, wrote down the address, and ripped a page out of the notepad, and handed it to him.

"Here you go, John. Say hello to Carolyn for me."

"Carolyn," the freak said, like a robot.

She looked at him oddly. "That's Mrs. Hawk's name."

"I always call her Mrs. Hawk."

"You call your aunt Mrs. Hawk?"

The suit ignored her, just turned and cleared out, leaving her there, looking even stupider than usual. Troy followed.

In the hallway near the exit, the aggressive kid wearing the earbuds was standing with a gang of other guys, making fun of the ugly girls passing by. But when the freak approached, he got quiet and turned away.

Okay, enough of this crap, thought Troy.

He rushed forward, planting himself between the freak and the doorway "Hey, tell me where I can get some threads like that, man…"

"Let me pass."

"Over my dead body."

The face in the navy-blue suit turned to look at him. He took a deep breath and blinked. Troy knew he had made a mistake, as he felt something wrap around his neck and tighten, then tighten more, and tighten even more. There was no one near him, but he felt like he was being choked to death.

Jesus, he thought, *I can't breathe. I'm gonna die.*

The freak smiled at him, waved and walked out of the school. Troy heard a gurgling sound coming from his own mouth. The world swirled and churned and turned black.

CHAPTER FIVE

O nce I'd accepted Cy's invitation, the danger really
began. I followed Cy a few more steps to the back of
the cave. He'd brought a flashlight, and as he waved
it around, the beam roved across the inner surface of the cave. I
noticed some smooth edges around a rock in the lower corner.
It looked like somebody had purposely sized it to fit in this
little space.

"What is that?"

Cy handed me a small garden shovel. "If you want knowledge, push that rock aside." I began to scrape around the edges
of the rock. Soon I could wiggle the rock, so I took out my
knife and wedged it and the shovel on either side of the rock.
With great effort, I was able to pop out the rock.

Behind the rock was a dark hole, about the width of a human
body. I crouched down and peered inside. Damp air poured
out from the hole, cooling my skin. Goosebumps appeared on
my neck and arms.

"What's down there?" I asked.

"I don't know," Cy replied, "but I have an idea. And it's very special."

"You never tried to get in?"

He sighed. "Sonny and I have spent our whole lives trying to find this. Our ancestors told us about it, but we didn't have the location. We just discovered it a few weeks ago."

"And the problem is that you can't fit," I said.

He shook his head. "But you—*you* could fit."

I looked down at my own torso. I wasn't very big, not like some of the other guys who I knew. I'd always wished I'd had a bigger ribcage, but now it looked like my physique might come in handy.

"Are you sure I won't get stuck?"

"No," he said, "but if you get stuck, I promise to help you out. Here, wear this."

From his bag he lifted a long length of rope and handed me one end. He hung it around my hips. I looked down at the old native American. "You were hoping I would follow you, weren't you?"

He looked up at me and grinned.

He finished tying the rope onto me, then handed me the flashlight. Then he unslung his backpack and said, "I brought some things that you might need. And one more thing."

"What?"

"When you get into the cave, don't touch the walls."

I scrunched up my face. "Don't touch the walls?"

"Trust me."

I agreed. At that point, I got onto my knees and crawled into the tunnel. I discovered that there was barely enough room for me to squeeze through. I threw the bag a few feet in front of me, crawled to catch up to it, and continued the process.

My back scraped against the rough surface of the tunnel. My knees were crying for relief.

After a minute, I heard Cy's distant voice behind me say, "You okay down there?"

"I guess."

I pushed forward, on hands and knees, pushing the bag, trying to control my breathing, trying to stuff down the panic. I thought about how strong professional spelunkers had to be. This was the most grueling thing I'd ever endured.

Suddenly I reached a portion of the tunnel that was impossibly small. It was almost exactly as wide as I was, and only a few inches higher. I knew that if there was any hope of getting through, I had to be fast. I put my arms in front of me, into the short passage, took a deep breath and exhaled until my lungs were totally empty. Then I began to make small rippling movements with my body, like like I was doing the caterpillar that people used to do on dance floors.

Just when the claustrophobia grew almost unbearable, and my lungs shouted for oxygen, the tunnel widened. I got to my hands and knees and stayed there for a moment, breathing like a dog. I wiped the sweat off my face with the sleeve of my shirt.

"William?" came Cy's distant voice.

"I'm still going," I said, "but this is really hard."

I started moving again, and the tunnel widened a little more so that I could crouch. Another minute of awkward hunched-over stumbling, and I felt the tunnel open up into a large room. It was nearly pitch black. I stood up fully and turned on the flashlight and looked around.

This was it.

To my amazement, I saw that the walls were covered with symbols, words and pictures. None of it was familiar. What was this place? Was it some kind of burial chamber? A place of worship? I got the distinct hairs-standing-on-the-neck feeling that I wasn't supposed to be in here.

I remembered the backpack. I looked inside, and in addition to a first aid kit and a bag of peanuts and some water, I found a notepad and a nub of a worn-out pencil.

I positioned my flashlight on a rock and pointed it at one wall. Then I sat down, and, using the pencil, I began to jot down the symbols as best I could. I wanted to show them to Cy. I was sure he would have some insight.

When I was finished, I crawled back down the tunnel the same way I'd come in. It was slightly easier the second time, because at least I knew what to expect. I walked out of the cave, blinking in the brightness, momentarily blinded. Then I saw Cy. He'd built a small fire at the mouth of the cave. He had speared a small animal of indeterminate origin and was cooking it over the flames.

He looked up as I came over. "I got us some squirrel to eat."

"Yummy. Hey, you're not going to believe what I found."

Cy turned the animal over to its other side. "You have to be very careful not to overcook squirrels. You go a minute or two over, and it could burst into flames. It nearly took the eyebrows off my face."

"Enough about the squirrel," I said. Handing the notebook to him, I open to the scribbled pictures and symbols. He forgot about the roasting animal and stepped away from the fire, seemingly captivated by what I had just shown him.

Finally, he cleared his throat. "Where did you find this?"

"This is what's in that cave. There are huge drawings all over the walls."

We talked for several more minutes about the different symbols and pictures I had seen. I could tell that he was legitimately impressed.

"What is that place?" I said.

"Our ancestors called it the Hall of Knowledge," he said softly. "Many others have searched far and wide for that room. It's said to contain many mysteries of the universe. But I wouldn't know for sure unless I could get in myself."

I seized him by the arm. "Oh, you could. We could buy a few small sticks of dynamite and…"

"No, no, we can't damage anything. It's a sacred place."

I was struck by the way he said that. *Sacred.*

Suddenly there was a loud explosion from the fire. I jerked down instinctively and covered my face. When I uncovered my eyes, Cy had raced over and was frantically beating the squirrel with a towel. It had burst into flames.

"You distracted me," he said. "Anyway, we'll come back tomorrow."

The next morning Cy was up before the sun. From my mattress, I cracked open an eye and watched him gather tools, water bottles, drawing pads, and other things. He wasn't being very quiet about it either.

"I guess it's time to get up," I said.

He kept puttering around. "I made us a couple sandwiches. You're going to be busy today."

"Doing what?"

"Drawing."

As he continued, I understood what he wanted me to do. I was to copy the rest of the symbols on the walls as closely as possible, so that he could see them all.

As we walked with the equipment, there was no doubt that Cy was excited to get back to the cave. It was as though he had waited his whole life for this event—which, in fact, he had. On the way, he couldn't stop talking about ancient mysteries, symbols that predicted the future, and prophecies being fulfilled. I wasn't skeptical, just confused—the symbols hadn't made any sense to me.

Luckily, it was a cool morning, and the sun was just starting to heat up our shoulders when we arrived at the cave around mid-morning. He began unloading the packs and laid out all the supplies on the floor. I noticed there was a roasting pan among them. It was looped to a long rope with two pulleys at each end.

"Cy, what are you going to do with that?"

He put his hands on his hips. "That's going to be our trolley. We'll put the materials into the pan and pass them back and forth. Sound good?"

"I guess so."

Cy tied one end of the long rope to my belt and handed me a pulley. "Now, crawl down that tunnel. When you arrive, I'll start passing you the equipment through the tunnel. Then you make the drawings."

I obliged and got down on my hands and knees and crawled down the tunnel for the second time, feeling the cool, damp air on my face. Once I'd arrived in the cave, I shouted back to him.

"Ready," his voice said.

I cranked the pulley. The sound of a heavy pan clattering down the tunnel reached my ears. I kept turning the crank.

"That'll wake the dead for sure," I said.

The pan arrived. It was loaded with tools. After several trips with the jerry-rigged trolley, we had moved everything into the room. We had to get the images in the cave the old-fashioned way, but I wanted to approach it systematically. First, I used string and bits of gum to draw a temporary grid, eight by eight, across the symbols on the walls. Then I drew out a similar grid on the paper that we'd brought. Following that, I squatted and began to draw each symbol with its location and grid number.

It was a painstaking process. The room was full of more information than we could possibly imagine. Every half hour or so, I sent the trolley back to Cy with several sheets of paper. I tried to draw the best representation possible. I heard him grumbling to himself, almost as if he were arguing back and forth with an imaginary person. Sometimes he instructed me to look more closely and report back what I found. As I drew them, I felt that many of the inscriptions on the walls seemed familiar, but I wasn't sure how I could've known them. I noticed the repetition of certain symbols and the order in which they were aligned; these were likely clues to their meaning.

It turned out that one day wasn't enough to capture everything. The cave was extensive, and I was the only one who could fit inside. For the next week, Cy and I spent every day repeating the same process. In the evenings, we returned to the cabin, trying to evaluate my drawings with a fine-toothed comb—how they all fit together and what the meaning could be. The work felt endless and seemed futile, and it didn't seem that we were making any progress, but maybe I didn't have the right perspective. Cy had insights that I didn't, but he couldn't get a sense of the cave as a whole, not even from my precise drawings.

On the fifth day, I was deep into my drawing of panel twenty-seven when I heard someone call my name.

William.

I put down my pencil and lifted my head and looked around. There was nobody else in this cave. Just the single light that I'd set up, the duffle bag with the other supplies, the remains of my lunch.

William.

I felt myself getting sleepy. I stretched myself out on my back on the cave floor and shut my eyes.

That's when she appeared.

A stunning girl is walking toward me across a meadow. She's tall, with hair past her shoulders, and moves in as though there were no atmosphere around her, no ground beneath her feet.

William, she says.

Yes?

Come rescue me. We have things to do.

What things?

You'll see me, but I won't be able to speak.

But where?

I'll be still. Find me.

Then the image liquefied and faded, and I woke up. I found myself in the cave again.

I sat up. I realized that the dream hadn't been coincidental, or random, like so many normal dreams. That girl had *contacted* me, clearly and telepathically—and I suspected that it was because of either my new powers or this location. Or both.

"What is your name?" I asked out loud.

The word came into my head loud and clear. *Grace.* Then she was gone again.

Her name was Grace.

I picked up the notepad again and continued drawing. Getting through this project and learning as much as I could about my new altered reality was the best way for me to find her.

Grace.

I repeated her name, tasting it on my lips until I finished, and crawled back through the tunnel to Cy.

✧✧✧

The next morning, I wondered about this girl. Grace. I knew, of course, that it could have been just a dream, my imagination running unchecked by my subconscious mind. But, no. That had been no dream. I didn't know what it was, but it was no dream. I knew she had come to me, that she was real, that she needed me. How? I suppose the same way that any of us "know" what "real" is or was. If yesterday you went to the movie with your girlfriend, well, you'd know that this was somehow a different, more "real" experience than when you dreamed last night that you were being chased by a unicorn. You just know.

I was packing the duffel bag for the day when Cy came over to me. "I have a better idea," he said.

"What is it?" I asked.

"We're not going to the cave today."

I looked up at him. "But I'm not done yet."

"I know. But I want to see what you see, in proportion. So, I have an idea."

I'm a big fan of thinking outside the box, but it turned out that Cy's newest idea involved staying inside of it.

We drove to the little village in the center of the reservation. There was a sad little market on a corner that was sad in that hopelessness seemed heavy in those milling around.

"What are we doing here?" I asked.

"We're getting their cardboard," he said.

I let that one twist around my brain while he pulled up behind the store. There was a deli worker sucking on a cigarette next to the dumpster. Cy rolled down his window and said some words in his native language. The worker just pointed toward a stack of flattened boxes wound up in twine, and then returned to his love affair with his cigarette.

"Would you mind?" Cy asked me.

I stepped out of the vehicle and nodded to the deli worker. He didn't notice me. I picked up the bale of cardboard and hauled it to Cy's truck and, with great effort, threw it in the back.

I climbed back into the truck. "Now you have to tell me why."

"We got to stop one more place," said Cy.

He drove us around to a little hardware store in the village. We went inside, and it smelled like stale cigarettes. I hung around the front of the store, close to the exit, while he collected a basket of duct tape, nails, wire and more rope. I wasn't sure what the old guy had in mind. However, it seemed as though he knew exactly what he was doing.

He paid for the items, and we returned to the truck.

"Cy," I said, "the suspense is killing me."

"I want to see what you see inside that room, and those are my materials."

It dawned on me what he was planning to do. "You're going to build a replica of the cave."

"Yes. I'm going to put your drawings on the walls. And then I can sit inside of it."

That was fairly ingenious, but I wondered again, "Shouldn't we just dynamite your way in?"

He gave me a look, and I raised my hands in surrender.

At the cabin, we wordlessly began to clear out all the furniture from inside.

"This is like what we used to do when we were kids," he said.

"Yeah," I said, "I used to build a fort in the fields behind my house."

It turned out that the project took us almost two days, and the cabin was only big enough to give us a three-foot perimeter around the cardboard walls, but it worked. We assembled all the cardboard with the duct tape, rope and wire. We built a couple of duct-tape hinged doors that gave us access to the center of the room. Then we attached all my drawings to the walls.

Finally, we stood back and admired our handiwork. Cy dragged a chair into the middle of the room, parked himself in it, and stared at the completed walls.

"Do you want my help?" I asked.

Cy waved the question off. I could see him starting to enter a trance. I quietly stole out of the room and went for a walk in the woods and sat down on a granite outcropping. I watched a squirrel carry an acorn into the hollow of a tree. He was building something too. There didn't seem to be anything for me to do. Cy could access his people's ancient knowledge, and I could not.

So, I waited.

CHAPTER SIX

Deputy Hanson kept an eye on Sheriff Winters, who stood in front of the map. He jabbed a thick finger at the map. "Here, or here, or here, or here. He could be any of these places."

"We looked, Sheriff," said Hanson.

"We couldn't find him," said Deputy Small, who mostly stared at the half a sandwich on his desk.

"What about the bus driver?"

"He already told us everything," Hanson told the sheriff, which annoyed him, as he had already told the sheriff that. "He got out on Old Nicholson Road and said he didn't know where he was going. That was the last anybody saw of him."

"So he's either dead or he hitched a ride."

"Or both. Not in that order, probably."

"What does state have?"

Hanson shrugged. "States have nothing. Not one lead. Hey, Chief, I know this is your daughter's boyfriend and all, but why are we even bothering? It was a harmless fight between two kids."

Sheriff Winters punched a hand into his fist. "Boys, normally I am not so, shall we say, *demonstrative*. But this kid was my daughter's new boyfriend. He assaulted my nephew, and it could've just as easily been her." He emphasized every word of the next sentence slowly. "I…want…William…Hawk… locked up."

"Yes, sir," replied both deputies at the same time.

Hanson thought the boss was losing it. The sheriff had always been an odd duck, no doubt there, but he seemed to be getting even odder.

"Now go find him," the sheriff ordered. He reached for a piece of hard candy, unwrapped it with a crinkle, popped it in his mouth and grinned, then pointed toward the door. On his left hand was the faded remnant of a cross, something he never seemed to want to discuss when Hanson asked about it.

CHAPTER SEVEN

The old man's trance lasted three days. I didn't see him eat anything, I didn't see him sleep, I didn't see him do anything. He didn't even answer when I crouched down next to him and tried to speak to him. He just looked at the walls, occasionally murmuring to himself.

On the third morning, he got up and began writing on the drawings in red pencil. I stood over him and looked down. He was adding extra symbols in the white spaces.

Then he put down the pencil and looked at me. "It's time to go back."

"Where?"

An odd light was burning in his eyes. "To the Hall of Knowledge. You're going to tell me if this is right." He handed me the drawings, and I put them in the bag.

When we arrived at the cave, there was a mystical feeling in the air, a presence that I had not been aware of before. Setting up our equipment and our little trolley as we had in the past went much quicker this time. I crawled quickly down the tunnel—it was getting easier. Once inside the cave, the first thing I did was unroll the three pages that we brought from the cabin. Cy had added, in red pencil, the extra symbols that he thought belonged in the blank space.

I looked at the sheets and matched up the grid work I had laid out earlier. Sure enough, on the walls were the symbols that Cy had sketched. They were faint, blending in quite well with the natural texture of the cave walls

I leaned down to the mouth of the tunnel and said, "You were right."

A whoop sounded from the far end of the tunnel. "I knew it. Come back out here so we can talk."

I made my way back out of the tunnel. The journey on hands and knees had grown much easier.

When I returned, Cy pulled me outside into the bright sunlight. There, with the valley spread out around us, he placed his hands on my shoulders. "My ancestors have passed down stories since the beginning of time. They told of a place where the great knowledge keeper stored a record of every Ignition. Many generations of seekers have been searching for this room, but no one has been able to find its location."

"Well, you did."

He nodded. "The Great Spirit has chosen us to reveal it. You and me."

I stood there, looking at him, trying to take this in. "I want to know more."

We sat down on a nearby rock. He began to speak: "The Great Spirit shared a story with my forefathers. It told of a family consisting of ten brothers that left their family to embark on a journey of enlightenment. They were to discover and understand the principles needed to achieve a flourishing humanity.

Legend has it that one named Apollyon, an Under Lord, rose up against the great Spirit, El-Elyon. He did not want to follow in the ways of old, but instead wanted to elevate self above all things. He would do anything to deceive and twist the ways of El-Elyon. The challenge to the ten brothers was to resist the darkness and become one with the light, but the path that each of these brothers chose has been as varied as the clouds in the sky. As each civilization reached its final ignition point, Apollyon and his legions of deceivers were forced to leave, but they continue to transport themselves to the next civilization."

I interrupted, "But what does it *mean?*"

"It means that we are leading up to the greatest battle. At the end, all of Apollyon's forces will be gathered in one place. I fear that our earth has become the battlefield."

He paused, pointed to the symbol on my hand. "That's a symbol of the role you're going to play in the battle. It's on the wall."

I shot to my feet.

"Hang on," he said.

"I need to look at it again."

Then I felt myself get down on hands and knees and scamper back quickly into the inner sanctum.

Inside, I stood up and looked around with new eyes. I experienced a flash of insight, almost as if a set of blinders had come off. The room began to make sense. The wall on the left consisted of ten columns, and at the top of each was a symbol. I looked more closely. Those symbols suddenly seemed familiar, and then I remembered why.

I'd seen them on my birthday—that moment when everything had changed.

I studied the ten columns more closely. Each column represented information pertaining to that symbol, and the same symbol crowned the top of each of the first seven columns. Underneath each of those seven columns was etched a date.

Cy had used that phrase *final ignition point* to mean the date at which a civilization fought against Apollyon, and rose up.

It seemed that three of the ten civilizations hadn't done that yet. I turned my attention to those three.

My eyes fell upon the tenth and final column. I noticed that the symbol at the top looked familiar. It was a cross. I looked down at my left hand.

I sat down suddenly. My head was swimming. This cave may have been called the Hall of Knowledge by Cy's ancestors, but I was feeling less knowledgeable than ever. There was apparently an entire world separate from our world—and I had been given access to it. Cy had been right. This room was trying to tell me something. Our civilization hadn't reached its final ignition point, not yet. And I was going to have something to do with it when it happened.

William, where are you? a voice asked.

It was Grace. Again.

I shot to my feet and stared at the wall, sweat at my temples and lips pursed tight. That wasn't my imagination. She was here again, guiding me. I quickly went to the wall. In that instant, I realized that I hadn't physically touched any of the symbols yet. I guess I was afraid of damaging the relic or intruding on something holy and sacred, as Cy had seemed to think. Or maybe I was afraid of what I would get myself into.

I felt myself reach out and touch the wall—and a pulse of energy swept through my body, knocking the breath out of me and sending me three steps backward. When I'd recovered, I looked at the wall where my fingers had touched, and I was shocked at what I saw. There were two little figures, each with their right hand extended. On each hand was a mark.

It was the same mark that I had on my hand.

The word *William* had been etched near one figure. It hadn't been there before. Beneath the other was the word *Grace*. That hadn't been there either.

Between them, I watched two more words slowly etch themselves into the rock.

Find me.

It was too much. I suddenly felt the urge to get out. I scrambled back through the tunnel, got to my feet, and ran out of the cave. I could hear Cy shouting behind me. I didn't care.

This was too much.

CHAPTER EIGHT

W illiam's mother stood over the pot of soup in the kitchen. She had just finished adding the chicken, vegetables, broth, spices. Now there was nothing left for her to do but wait for everything to come together.

The same as she was doing for her son.

They hadn't heard a word from William. They had heard all about what he'd *done*—the incident in the sporting goods store, the bus ride, and the silence ever since. Sheriff Winters, Julia's father, had come and spoken with them. They'd been unable to find him.

At first, they had gone driving aimlessly, putting up missing signs at gas stations, convenience stores, post offices. They had canvassed the area for fifty miles in every direction. Nothing came of it. It was as though William had simply vanished off the face of the earth.

Now her husband had withdrawn into his workspace in the garage. He was in there for hours every night. When she asked what he was working on, he said it was a project for William.

It was something William had asked for, maybe something that had to do with his disappearance. He refused to say any more. William's mother was just as clueless as everybody else.

She felt the tears starting to come. It was the fourth time today. She let them come, because nothing was going to stop them, not until there was some resolution, knowing if William was either alive or dead.

The doorbell rang. She reached for a paper towel and wiped her cheeks. She checked her face in the bathroom mirror before heading to the front door.

She saw a boy about William's age, a strange boy, in a navy-blue pinstripe suit with dress shoes that glinted in the light over the doorway. He wore a crooked grin, like he had never smiled before and was faking it.

"Carolyn Hawk?" he asked.

"Yes," she said.

"My name is John Patience. I'm a friend of William's from school, and I have some good news about your son."

She clapped a hand to her mouth. "Oh my gosh. Let me get my husband. Can you wait just one second?"

The grin grew tighter. "May I come in?"

"Of course." William's mother unlocked the clasp. When she turned around she felt as though she had been punched in the back, and when she reached behind, her back was wet.

That was strange, she thought. When she looked at her hand, it was covered in blood.

CHAPTER NINE

I woke up the next morning and heard Cy grumbling and talking to himself in the middle of the cardboard room. He was pointing to some symbols that were up above the ten identifying marks and mumbling to himself.

"Cy," I said.

"Yes, William."

I paused. "This place is really getting to me."

"I figured as much," he said.

"None of this can be true. You drugged my oatmeal."

He grinned. "Oh, it's real, and I've been waiting for this moment for years. Sonny and I uncovered it, but neither of us could fit inside, and neither of us trusted anybody else enough to confide in. Then you showed up. Not a coincidence."

I stretched out. "So how would you describe the Hall of Knowledge in one sentence?"

"The Hall of Knowledge is a repository for the ever-changing knowledge of the ten brothers."

"Which are representative of civilizations."

"Yes. My ancestors spoke of it. They described how every full moon the brothers changed the symbols. In that way, the brothers can share advances and rely on one another."

I liked the way he kept saying *brothers* when what he meant was *civilizations*. But this wasn't the time to admire his metaphors.

Cy continued: "The big pitfall however is that it's become more difficult for the brothers to communicate. The more each brother turns inward, neglecting the other brothers, the harder it is to do so."

I couldn't hold back my story any longer. "I touched the wall, Cy."

"And?"

"And it formed my name. And another name."

"Whose?"

I continued the story, telling him about how Grace came to me in the hall.

He was silent, then said, "The wall needs to be touched in a certain way to access this knowledge. The mind has to be open, the fruit ripe. It seems that you have all that. It is what opened up your mind to the possibility of what this chamber can do. Come outside. I have something else to tell you."

I groaned and pulled on my pants. The day was rainy and overcast, and we stood together in the middle of the pine grove. He faced me. His expression was serious.

"I know that you find me mysterious," he said.

"Who wouldn't?"

"I haven't been direct with you because I was trying to figure out what level you were at. But now I know." He paused. "You're a Change Agent."

"I'm a what, now?"

"A person that has the potential for bringing good change.

We're all Change Agents, actually. There are three levels. Let me explain."

Cy collected six pine cones. He picked up the first pine cone. "Change Agent 1 is an ordinary person. Most humans are at this level. They will not influence evil on their planet, but they will also only inspire minor amounts of good. C.A. 1s have no real discernable powers and do not remember the parallax except in short, unexplainable spurts – if at all."

Then Cy picked up the group of two pine cones. "A Change Agent 2. They have some powers and are expected to work toward moderate levels of good. They can sense other Change Agents, but they don't communicate telepathically or control others' emotions. They also remember the parallax."

"I'm still confused."

Cy waved it off. "Later." Then he picked up the group of three pine cones. They filled his hands. "Then we have Change Agent 3. These unique individuals are designated with an ability to achieve the highest level of skill on their planet and obtain full memory of the parallax. These individuals work toward significant good. They can share thoughts with each other telepathically and exude emotions on others."

He fixed his eyes on me. "Based on what happened in the cave, tell me which one you seem to be."

I gulped. "A C.A. 3?"

Cy nodded. "Before you go getting a big head, you should know something else. C.A.3s are highly susceptible to falling into evil." He dropped all the pine cones onto the ground. I looked at his empty hands. "That's what we call a C.A. 0."

"Change Agent 0."

He nodded. "A C.A. 0 has turned his back on all that is good. For example, Adolf Hitler was a C.A. 3, but he decided to go down the path of evil. Boom. He fell down to zero."

He clapped an arm across my shoulders. "I felt this from you from the moment I picked you up on the road. In fact, something was telling me to drive on that road that night."

"I don't think I'm meant for big things."

"Oh, you are. Just got to accept that, William."

I decided to change the subject. "What about you? Where are you on that scale?"

"I'm a C.A. 2. So is Sonny. That's why we're trying to help you through the transition. We understand better than the C.A. 1s."

I stepped back with my hand against my forehead. This hurricane of revelations needed to stop. I'd seen movies—I don't know, like *Spiderman*—where some average schmo gets superpowers and is supposed to fight evil. Was I another Peter Parker? That was the stuff that serious nut jobs thought. Was I now a serious nut job?

Cy spoke up again. "Now, the last surprise for the day."

"Seriously?"

"I've been looking at the symbols all night, matching up lunar with celestial cycles, and the ancestors helped me understand that a significant date is coming up."

"When?"

"Saturday."

"What's going to happen?"

He grew concerned and stroked his chin. "I'm not exactly sure. My guess is that something is going to enter this Hall of Knowledge and change the columns. The walls act kind of like a billboard. They get changed every so often, but I don't know exactly what gets changed or why."

It sounded a little crazy to me. "Did you sleep at all last night?"

He just gave me a little shake of his head, indicating no. That was no surprise. His cheeks were looking very drawn, his chunky butt seemed to have vanished, and his potbelly wasn't quite so pot anymore.

Then he clapped his hands together. "So that gives us three days to draw the rest of the walls. If I'm right about this date, we need to record as much as we can before Saturday. Let's go!"

In the cave, I got inside the inner sanctum and set up the lights and looked around. I didn't have the papers yet—they were on the trolley behind me—but nothing seemed amiss.

At the other end of the tunnel, Cy said, "Is there anything that looks different to you?

"No, not yet."

"Good, that means my math was right. Get to work!"

For the next three days, I eagerly produced page after page of the walls. I worked feverishly, making sure not to disturb any symbols. Every half hour, like some Renaissance artisan in the service of some greater project, I put my finished sketches onto the pan, with the square neatly labeled in the upper left corner, and shouted to Cy to pull it down the tunnel.

I drew not just the ten columns, but also the hundreds of other seemingly random symbols that decorated the walls. It may have been my exhaustion, but somehow I began to understand the symbols—and the stories that Cy had shared with me finally became more understandable. It was evident to me that the forces of darkness were impacting civilizations evermore strongly, causing them to turn in upon themselves, stunting their inhabitants' souls.

As I scribbled furiously, I occasionally heard her calling me. *William, find me.*

I will, Grace, I answered.

By Friday, I had completed everything. Meanwhile, Cy had developed the enthusiasm of a little kid. He'd mounted the missing pieces on the wall of the replica room, not even stopping for meals. I watched him analyzing my handiwork, wondering how long it would be before he had another epiphany.

"I'm off to bed," I said.

"Me too," said Cy, "just as soon as I study this a bit more."

"What can we expect tomorrow?" I asked.

He smiled mysteriously. "Let's leave it until then."

As I fell asleep, he was still staring at the replicated walls.

CHAPTER TEN

Deputy Hanson found Sheriff Winters filling his coffee cup at the beverage station in the office, about to dump creamer in. Hanson couldn't quite believe what he had just seen, and his stomach churned.

"Boss, we got a problem at the Hawks'. A big one."

He sipped his coffee. "What did he do now?"

Hanson tried to keep his hands from shaking. "We gotta get over there."

Thirty minutes later, Hanson waited as Sheriff Winters stood outside the bedroom, looking at the butchered body of Carolyn Hawk. There was a blood spot on her back and several slashes across her hands and wrists, indicating that she was trying to protect herself when the killer moved in to finish her off.

The sheriff turned to the left. On the floor near the bedroom door was the butchered body of her husband. His wounds were fewer but worse—one deep wound in the abdomen and another across the throat. He probably bled out relatively quickly. The woman, on the other hand, had lived much longer. The brother was at the bottom of the steps, practically decapitated.

Hanson asked what had to be asked. "You think it was the boy?"

"Probably showed up out of the blue, and when the parents got angry, junior hacked them to bits."

Hanson had asked around quite a bit about the kid lately. No one had a bad word to say about the boy, except the cousin who had his butt whipped in the store. But, Hanson thought, maybe the kid was on the reefer or something.

The sheriff slapped his thigh. "I want every neighbor interviewed, every road covered. I want a hotline set up. William Hawk must be found before he carves anybody else up into mincemeat."

"We don't have evidence, do we? I mean, except that he is their kid and that he took off?"

"Well, we can pick him up for assault, then we can find the murder evidence. Okay?"

CHAPTER ELEVEN

Next morning, as the sun started to peek through the window, I woke up with a start. The cabin was completely silent. No rustling, grumbling, clanging. Typically Cy was about as quiet as a falling stack of crockery in the morning.

He wasn't here. I walked outside, checked the privy. Nothing. Then I scanned the hillside. Cy was nowhere to be found.

It was possible he went to town, but not likely, since today was Saturday. No, he had gone to the cave without me. That was odd, because all he could do was stand there and look at the mouth of the tunnel.

Or so I'd been led to believe.

I got dressed and went running down the path and made it to the cliff in half the usual time. I let myself down the ropes and was breathing heavily by the time I stepped into the cave.

It was empty, but the rock that covered the tunnel had been pushed aside. That was strange, since I always closed it tight every night when I left. Either someone else had discovered this place—which was not likely—or Cy had done something quite rash.

I had to find out, so I got down on hands and knees and proceeded to slide through the tunnel. I hit the tight midpoint, the part where I always had to suck in my breath, and noticed something odd.

A strip of ripped fabric in the dirt. It was white cotton and appeared to have been part of a T-shirt. Cy had been wearing a white T-shirt when I went to sleep last night.

I crawled even faster through the last part of the tunnel. I saw a strange glowing light inside the Hall of Knowledge, and goose bumps ran up and down my spine. He'd been right about Saturday.

"Cy?" I shouted. "Are you here?"

I emerged into the Hall of Knowledge. The spooky greenish light was hovering near the ceiling like a malevolent mist. Somehow it seemed familiar. Then it vaporized nearly as soon as I entered.

And then I saw Cy.

The Native American was lying on his back in the middle of the space, his body equal distance from each of the four walls. He seemed totally exhausted, almost to the point of being unconscious. I knew he was old, but here he looked positively ancient. I wasn't sure if it was from the physical exertion of climbing through the tunnel, lack of food, or spiritual battles that he'd waged in here all night while I was asleep back at the cabin.

I rushed to his side. "Cy, how did you get in here?"

For some strange reason, when he opened his eyes, he had a little grin on his face. He pointed at his stomach. "I didn't eat. For weeks."

I thought about that. He had been making excuses about his meals the entire time that I'd known him—saying things like "I already ate" or "I'm not hungry." All excuses to squeeze himself into this cavern.

Then he put his index finger up and motioned for me to come closer.

"What?" I asked.

"I got the Proof that I needed."

I wasn't sure what he was talking about, but my mind instantly went back to the glowing light I had just seen.

"What was that light?"

A smile lit up his face. "It was the Great Spirit. It showed me the Proof."

"You're going to have to explain that to me," I said, "once I get you out of here."

"Why? I'm happy here."

"Because you look really bad."

"No," he said, "I don't want to leave."

I studied him. His fingernails were chipped and bleeding, his shirt was ripped, his belly scraped, the shallow but raw wounds red with blood. They were ripe for infection. He'd had a heck of a time squeezing in here. Still, he had that silly little grin on his face, like a kid who got caught with his hand in a candy jar. It was clear that this man would not have enough energy to get out on his own power.

"Cy, can you move?"

The old man tried to lift his arm. It fell back onto the rock, limp. "No, not at all."

I thought about that. Without Cy's cooperation, there would be no way that I could help him out of that tunnel. I sat back on my heels; I couldn't let Cy die in here, which is where it looked like things were heading. Then I hit upon a solution.

"Cy," I said, "don't move. I'll be right back."

✧✧✧

I headed out of the tunnel and then left the cave. I slid down the slope of the mountain until I reached the valley floor, where I sprinted until I suddenly ran into an invisible wall that knocked me off my feet.

Not you, said a voice.

Sprawling in the dirt, I looked around. I was alone. Then I recognized where I was. I had tried to run into the open stretch of land that Sonny had told me was the graveyard of his ancestors.

He'd been right. I wasn't welcome there.

I stood up, tried to walk forward again. I ran again into an invisible force field that prevented me from entering. It felt like Plexiglas. I decided to retrace my steps. I went back up the slope a little way, walked parallel with the graveyard, and then came down the slope at a point a little farther along. I crossed the valley without any trouble and clambered up the opposite slope.

As I approached Sonny's house, I found him in his rocking chair on the porch, watching me as I sprinted up. He was the type of guy who always waited for you to speak first, which put you at a disadvantage.

"Sonny," I said, "we have a problem."

He pointed out at the horizon. "Sun's comin' up in the east and settin' in the west."

"Listen, Cy is in trouble, and I need your help. He's in the cave."

Sonny looked up at me. His eyes were distant, and his heavy eyebrows looked like they were about to fall over his face.

"The cave."

"*That* cave," I said, hoping he understood my insinuation. "By the crescent moon rock. The Hall of Knowledge."

Sonny understood. "I told Cy when I found it, the Great

Spirit warns our people to avoid looking into such things."

I shrugged and didn't say anything. He glanced at my dirty hands and knees.

"And today is a special day. It's a day of reset."

I went on to explain what we had been doing. When I finished, he said, "You want me to help pull him out?"

"Yes."

"That could be hard."

I didn't say anything to that. Then I explained the situation about the narrow tunnel, Cy starving himself. Sonny shrugged, wiped his hands on a rag that was stuffed in his pocket. The smell of turpentine reached my nostrils.

"Well, maybe we can slide him out. But I'll need to take the car." He nodded toward his car, something from the fifties, a Chevrolet with big fins on the back, turquoise green, and in good shape, considering.

"That's fine."

We slid into Sonny's car. For the next half hour, it chugged along like an old John Deere tractor. I think it had never been tuned, but it kept on going. We drove around to the other side of the canyon. There was no road except an overgrown cat track. Somehow that old land yacht rumbled through the forest, branches whipping at the sides of the vehicle. It was as if Sonny had discovered a path that no one else knew of. At times, it felt as though we would slide right off the cliff.

After we had rolled down the valley, we chugged up and around by Cy's cabin. Then we went down to the rock plateau above the cave, this time without a road at all.

"I'm going to call this car the billy goat," I said.

"It is surefooted."

At last we made the final turn, and we pulled up onto the plateau from which the rope ladder swung. Sonny parked the vehicle, keeping the motor running, and exited. I did the same.

Slowly I inched to the edge. I wasn't particularly fond of heights, and right there below me was the mouth of the cave. Sonny went around to the trunk of his car, pulled a rope out of the back, and motioned for me to tie it around my waist.

"All due respect, Sonny," I said, "but what do you have in mind?"

In response, he pointed to the trailer hitch on his car. There was a winch attached to it. I watched him position the car, made sure the rope was connected securely to me, and made sure we took all the slack out of the rope before I started traversing over the edge.

The descent went quickly—I leaped off the side of the cliff, Sonny used the winch to pay out the rope; I returned to the wall a few feet lower and leaped off the wall again; Sonny paid it out again, and so on. Soon I felt my feet hit the ground in front of the entrance to the cave.

"William," he said.

I looked up. "What?"

"Catch," he said.

A large plastic bucket landed next to me. It was sealed shut. "What is this?"

"It's axle grease," he said. "I keep it in the trunk for the car. You'll need it to get him out."

Sonny was right. We couldn't squeeze him out without some sort of lubricant.

I darted inside the cave and put the axle grease inside the trolley pan. Then I peered into the tunnel. At the far end, that luminous aura had returned to the cavern. It wasn't natural, that was for sure.

"Cy!" I yelled, "we're here! To rescue you!"

Silence from inside the cavern. That was alarming. I got down on my hands and knees and quickly crawled through the tunnel into the cavern. When I arrived, he hadn't moved. This time, however, he was totally unconscious. The green light overhead didn't dissipate this time. It stayed there, unnatural, and as I pulled the trolley pan into the cave, I swear that I felt the light watching me.

At last the pan arrived. I opened the small tub and using my hands, covered his body in great globs of the grease. I turned him over and covered his backside too. When I was finished, I positioned him at the mouth of the tunnel. Then I untied the rope from around my own body and looped it several times around his torso, under his armpits, and between his legs. It wasn't professional, but it would work.

When he was ready, I picked up the rope and pulled it until it was tight. Then I gave it a few ferocious tugs. That was our agreed upon signal.

I thought I heard a faint shout outside the cave. Then the rope tightened even more. Far above us, Sonny was cranking the winch. Soon Cy's unconscious body moved a few inches, then another few inches. The plan was working.

I got down on my hands and knees and followed closely behind, cradling his head with my hand as much as possible. During the tight midpoint, Cy's belly scraped again along the roof of the tunnel. I heard him moan in pain.

"Almost out," I reassured him.

Finally, like a cork out of a champagne bottle, Cy popped out of the mouth of the tunnel. I came out after him. He was breathing hard now, fully awake, with some fresh blood on his belly and shoulders.

"Hang in there," I said.

I picked him up on my back and carried him a few yards out into the sunlight, though he was slippery as a fish.

"Sonny!" I shouted. "He's ready!"

I could hear the automobile start up, and Cy gave me a

weak thumbs up as his body was slowly cranked into the air. I watched him disappear over the lip of the cliff above me. A moment later, the rope came flying down again. I fastened it around my waist and then felt myself rising into the air.

CHAPTER TWELVE

A s I buried my head in my hands, I tried to remember the doctor's question, but my mind was an absolute jumble.

"Could you repeat the question?" I asked.

It'd been almost twenty-four hours since Sonny and I had rescued Cy from the Hall of Knowledge. We'd driven him back up to his cabin and laid him out on the mattress. I'd cooked some chicken broth and tried to feed him, but he wouldn't accept it. We'd both realized that he needed medical help.

So, we helped him stand and held his arms while he staggered outside into the passenger seat of his truck. I'd taken the keys, thanked Sonny, and turned the vehicle out of the sacred valley and back toward the nearest town and the hospital there. I was nervous driving, especially without a license. Like most kids, I had done it before, stupidly, but now I had had more reasons than ever to worry.

Now I was standing in the hallway of a hospital. The doctor, a middle-aged woman in a white coat, was looking at me with a neutral expression. A stethoscope was wrapped carelessly around her neck, and she held a clipboard and pen.

I hadn't been in civilization for a while. It felt strange, as though I were an astronaut who had reentered the troposphere.

She caught my attention. "I said, what is that stuff all over him?"

I finally came back to earth. "That's axle grease that I smeared all over him."

The doctor tapped her pen against her clipboard. "Do I want to know why?"

"Oh, I'll tell you. We wouldn't have been able to get him out of that cave without it. The tunnel was so small."

She tried to contain a smile. "You guys were having a lot of fun in the caves. What are you called? Spelunkers!"

"Yes, ma'am." Of course, it was not an option to tell her, or anybody, what we'd discovered.

"Do you know when was the last time Cy ate?"

I shrugged. "I've been living with him for about a month, and I don't remember seeing him eat anything for a few weeks."

The doctor's eyebrows nearly lifted off her face. "Do you know why?"

I shrugged again. "He doesn't explain himself to me."

She studied me. "How old are you?"

I thought just a beat and then said, "Nineteen."

"You two are a strange pair."

I didn't know what to say to that, so I didn't say anything. She turned to a nurse and barked an order to get an IV going. Then she turned back to me.

"We'll let you know as soon as we learn something further. Are you going to wait here?"

I didn't know. I didn't have any place else to go.

"I guess so," I said.

She pointed down the hall. "Waiting room is down there."

Another nurse escorted me to the waiting room. On the way, we passed the police officer on duty. He was reading the paper. He momentarily lowered his paper and glanced at me. That was the moment I remembered I was potentially a wanted man and started getting nervous. I flipped the hood of my sweatshirt over my head and went to a far corner of the waiting area and tried to hide myself behind a vending machine.

William, find me.

I must've passed out, because she spoke to me so clearly, it felt like she was whispering in my ear.

I'm here, Grace.

I bolted to my feet. Her voice was so loud, in a telekinetic sense, I knew that she was physically near. Could she be in this very hospital?

My hoodie safely over my head, I began to prowl the corridors of the hospital. I had my spiritual antenna up, waiting for a sign of life.

Find me, William.

I crisscrossed the second floor. I didn't see many patients, and the ones who were there didn't feel like Grace. They were mostly old people with oxygen tanks. Family members, including many children, were roaming the hallways. I remembered that it was Sunday, which meant that they'd come to visit grandpa or grandma. I had been gone so long that I'd nearly lost track of the days.

On the third floor, I passed several empty rooms. Then, at the end of the hallway, a single open door caught my eye. I felt something pulling me down the corridor, and I followed. My shoes made soft footfalls on the floor.

I'm here.

I arrived at the door and peered inside.

A young woman was lying in bed. The sheets had been pulled up around her chest and tucked in nicely. Her lustrous hair was brushed and spread out on the pillow around her head. She appeared to be about my age. She also appeared to be totally unconscious.

I knew it was Grace. There was no doubt. I knew it as surely as I knew my own name. But I needed to confirm.

At that moment, a pair of nurses walked by, chattering. They saw me peeking into the girl's room. Before they could demand to know why I was up here, I turned the tables on them.

"Ma'am," I said to the nearest nurse, "can you tell me, who is this girl?"

"I can't tell you that," she said. "That would violate patient confidentiality."

"But I think I might know her," I told her.

"Who are you?" she said, her eyes sizing me up. "Do you have relatives here?"

The other nurse laid a hand on the first one's arm. "Wait, Dolores, he said that he might know her." She turned to me, "What's her name?"

"I'm not sure," I said, "but I think I've seen her before. It might be Grace."

The nurses looked a little stunned by the news. I didn't know why that would give them pause. They should have her name from when she checked in.

"Should we tell him?" said the second.

The first one, Dolores, shrugged.

The second nurse joined me in the doorway. "She's a Jane Doe. We don't know who she is. She was brought in here, almost dead. She apparently had been bitten by a rattlesnake while she was out hiking, though we couldn't find any of the venom in her. She had a severe reaction to the medication we gave her and hasn't regained consciousness."

"Nobody's come to claim her either," said the other. "And her fingerprints aren't even in the database."

My mind reeled. Grace has been in a coma, bitten by a rattlesnake. It didn't really square with the way she'd been speaking to me. Or maybe it did.

"Is it okay if I go inside?"

The nurse looked nonplussed. "There's a policy against it." She eyed me suspiciously. "But if you can identify her, we'll stand out here in the hallway and wait." Then she added sternly, "No touching."

I entered the room, flipped my hoodie down, and approached Grace. Looking down on her, I began to feel the same thing I had felt inside the cavern, except this felt a little more personal—that same smattering of images went floating through my memory, the ones I'd had on my birthday, the ones that seemed quite vivid but foreign, as though they didn't belong to me. I couldn't be sure, but she sure had the same hair color, the same look as the girl in my visions.

I looked behind me and glanced at the nurses. They were talking to each other in low voices. I sneakily reached my hand out and touched the girl's arm.

William, you found me.

All those floating memories concentrated and leaped out of

the fog of memory, a thousand times more vivid. It *was* Grace. I knew that more certainly than I'd ever known anything before.

"No touching," said Dolores. I yanked my hand back and turned toward them. The nurses were staring oddly at me.

"Is your name William?" the second nurse said.

I felt my stomach drop to my shoes. I was a wanted man. I felt the sweat popping out all over my body. There was only one answer to that question—a lie. I was sorry for what had happened in the sporting goods store, but Julia's cousin wasn't seriously injured. I, meanwhile, had a far bigger problem to deal with.

"No," I lied. "I'm Fred."

"You look just like that boy who was on the news," she said. "The one who ran away. The one whose family…"

She trailed off, didn't finish the sentence. My stomach twisted itself into a thousand knots.

"Whose family did what?" I asked.

Dolores fixed me with a merciless stare. "Well, you're not him?"

"Nope."

"His family was killed yesterday. It's all over the news. Haven't you seen it?"

"No," I croaked. The room was going sideways. I struggled to keep myself from throwing up all over the place.

"Well, Grace is a good start," she said, turning away. "We'll check out the database." She left the room, and I stepped into the hall in a daze. I had the wherewithal to flip up my hoodie again as I went down the elevator, but otherwise I felt as though I had been struck by lightning.

My God, were they really all dead? My knees buckled, and this time I couldn't help it. I vomited on the elevator floor. I was wiping my mouth when the doors opened, and an older couple stood there, staring. I excused myself and pushed past them. I had to get out of there. That nurse might send someone after me. I stumbled through the front doors, crying, heartbroken. Could it be true? I had to know.

I don't remember the drive back to my hometown. I was catatonic, and again behind the wheel of Cy's truck. Still not caring that I didn't have a license.

When I pulled into my neighborhood, it was 4 p.m. My street was blocked off by a pair of sawhorses, and a police cruiser was parked behind them. A cop sat behind the wheel, looking down at something in his lap.

I felt cold sweat springing out all over my body. Those nurses couldn't have been referring to my family. They *couldn't* have been. But something had happened on my block.

I made an executive decision not to try turning down my street. It wouldn't be smart. The police could be looking for me. There could be a warrant out for my arrest. Instead, I would wait until nighttime.

I slunk down in the seat so that my face wasn't visible as I passed the roadblock. Then I turned out of the neighborhood, back onto the main road, and went to a park some ways away, where I stopped Cy's pickup under a tree and turned off the engine. I had nowhere else to go, not without risking discovery.

Then I sat there, frozen in fear, watching the sun sink lower on the horizon.

Six hours later, darkness had cloaked the park, and my armpits were damp with perspiration. I was still sitting in the truck. My body had been unable to move, but my mind had been spinning through the darkest possible scenarios.

Now I would do whatever it took to infiltrate my own house.

I started up the truck and drove back to the neighborhood. The sawhorses were still up, the cruiser still parked behind. I drove past them, circled a different block, and saw the other end of my street was similarly blocked.

There was only one way to do this—on foot.

I parked several blocks away, slipped out of the truck, put up my hood, and began crossing through the yards. It was pitch dark and my neighborhood had no streetlights, so it was easy to slink around undetected. After a few minutes, I arrived on my street. The two cruisers were at either end, and I was enveloped in darkness.

I turned to face my house. It was ringed with yellow crime-scene tape. All the lights were off.

I trembled. My knees went weak. What had happened here? The idea that my family could be dead was simply not something I could believe. There had to have been some kind of mistake, some incorrect identification of victims, something. What would I do without them? This was what real terror was, not some slasher movie that made murder a kind of entertainment.

I found my house key in my pocket, went around to the side of the house, ducked under the tape, and put the key in the side door. It opened like usual. I slipped inside the house.

It was dark and cold. There was dried-up food on the kitchen counter. I felt my way to the garage and found my father's flashlight and carefully began shining it around the house. I didn't dare turn on a lamp.

Then I saw it.

An enormous bloodstain on the living room carpet. There was a trail of blood that went from the front door to where the phone was kept in the kitchen. Another trail of blood led upstairs. I dropped to my knees, shaking, cold, in shock.

Then I heard a sound from the side door. I crawled behind the sofa.

"William?" said a woman's voice. It seemed familiar.

A silhouette against the darkness came into view. I squinted my eyes but stayed silent.

"Is that you?" she said.

I finally recognized her. It was Miss Camilla, my neighbor from across the street. She was wearing one of her strange outfits. But I wasn't sure if I should reveal myself, so I didn't move.

"Honey baby," she said, "I know you're here. I just want to tell you that there was a terrible event."

I knew what she was about to say before she said it, but I said it anyway. "What?"

"I'm sorry. Your family is dead."

CHAPTER THIRTEEN

I let out a muffled whimper and slumped against the wall. I felt that something in me changed at that moment—and it didn't have anything to do with Change Agents or First Activations or Great Spirits or ten civilizations. Any remnant of the carefree teenager who I'd once been had now evaporated. I was completely alone. What would I do? Where would I go? How would I face the world without my mother's strength and my father's guidance? And my brother, he had been just a kid, like me. Someone had taken everything from him.

Miss Camilla must've heard me, because the next thing I knew she was crouched at my side, putting her arm around me.

"I'm not going to ask you where you've been or what you've been doing, but you gotta know something. The police are looking *everywhere* for you."

I tried to focus. "They are after me for attacking Julia's cousin."

"No. Not that." Her tone told me more than her words did. The cops couldn't think *that*.

"Are they saying I did it? How could they think that?"

She nodded.

I was numb. Everybody thought I had killed my own family?

"Where did they take them?"

"Who?"

"The bodies."

She spoke softly. "I don't know where, but they took them out last night."

"I didn't do this," I said, burying my head in my hands.

Miss Camilla softened. "I know you didn't."

I lifted my head. "How do you know? Apparently, the world is looking for me!"

"Because I saw the one who did," she said.

I looked at her. She offered her hand. "Stand up. Let's go to my house, and I'll tell you more."

I had no place to go, no one to take care of me. Except this neighbor in a purple muumuu, Miss Camilla.

"Okay," I said.

We went out of my house by the side door and closed it and stole quickly across the darkened street. She hustled me around the rear of the house, away from any prying eyes that might be watching the front door. She quietly lifted one of the slanted bulkhead doors that led into her basement and gestured for me to enter. I gingerly went down the steps into the darkness.

She followed behind me and closed the doors, then locked them using a padlock. I stood there waiting for her, smelling some kind of spices and feeling the warmth of the place, in such contrast to my house, now a cold place of death and horror.

Then she lit a hurricane lamp and carried it into the middle of the room. It was beautifully decorated, with a pair of sofas, a small table, and a vintage turntable near the wall. There were long pieces of flowing fabrics everywhere—cast over the lamp shades, cascading down from bookshelves, pooled in the crevices of the sofa.

It wasn't just a basement; it was a refuge from the world.

"You're going to stay here," she said. "I can't let you upstairs because there have been officials coming in and out since yesterday. I think it's all finished, but you never know."

I sat down on the sofa and put my head in my hands. Miss Camilla's fingertips touching me lightly on the shoulders as she walked out of the room. She came back a few minutes later with a tray bearing a teapot, two mugs, and a tray of cookies.

She sat down opposite me in a club chair, poured the tea, sat back and regarded me. I knew that I looked horrible.

"Your parents didn't do anything wrong," she said.

I took a teacup with trembling hands. "Then who did it? And why?"

"A young man, about your age. He showed up on your front porch wearing a navy-blue banker's suit. He rang the doorbell. And they let him inside. Very unusual to see a young man in such an outfit nowadays."

"How do you know all this?" I asked.

"Because I like to watch what happens in this neighborhood, as you well know. It's my neighborhood, and it's my right." She paused. "I've also seen what your father has been doing in his garage workshop. Those helmets." She looked at me as if I should know what that meant.

My ears pricked up. "My dad wasn't working on any helmets."

"Sure he was. He's been going gung-ho on'em for the last month. I've been watching him out there, every night."

That made me think. First that he was gone, but second that he had been working on the idea that I'd given him. Maybe it was his way of trying to connect with me during the last month.

I sighed. "What do you think I should do about my parents? Should I let the authorities know that I wasn't here?"

"Well, they said you were up for that assault charge…"

My fingers gripped my teacup. "Who said that?"

"The anchorman on the news. He said it yesterday."

There was no way that I could turn myself in to the police, not if they were intent on pinning this on me. Which meant something else.

"I'm not going to be able to bury my parents," I said.

She didn't say anything to that. I felt myself losing control. The teacup dropped from my hands and fell onto the carpet and spilled. Miss Camilla didn't move. She knew just how I was feeling.

"There are no words," she said, "to express how you're feeling. It's going to take you a long time to come to grips with it."

I looked up at her with tear-stained cheeks, and then the anger in me began to flare. "I can find him. I *will* find him. And I will find out why he did this. And I will take revenge."

Standing in the shower later that night, crying, I washed off the accumulated dirt of all those weeks in the cabin. I couldn't, however, wash off the stain of the knowledge that my parents were dead. The pain would never come off.

Miss Camilla had brought me food, but I couldn't eat. I felt dissociated from my body. I toweled off and went to lay on the basement sofa, my new home. I fell asleep, which was surprising. This night, though, it seemed that something was drawing me out of consciousness.

My body has taken on a kind of transparent state. I sense everything around me, though I'm not sure how, since I don't have eyes, ears or fingers.

I find myself traveling through a material that appears to be a rock, soil or mineral formation. This most definitely is a different world from what I had experienced in any other dream or vision.

Drifting along, my essence eventually reaches the interior of this place, and the sense of traveling through some sort of material ends. For a moment, there is nothing but pitch black. Normally that could cause me to panic, but not here. Images form in my mind, perhaps via a chemical reaction, perhaps via a sonar imprint. It feels a lot like waves arriving onto the shore—when the wave first splashes against your toe, it has little impact. Step farther out into the surf, and the impact increases significantly. When you get out to waist-deep water, a wave can easily knock you over.

This is what I experience. This consciousness is vast in numbers, a multitude of beings, but still has a degree of independence. I use the word independence loosely as I never detect individuality. The farther I go into their world, the stronger they become in aggregate.

Then the temperament of the beings changes. They grow nasty and aggressive. I feel myself drowning under a wave of what seems like liquid evil. If I had lungs, I would be suffering horribly. As it is, the experience leaves an awful, bitter taste in my mouth.

Then the process works backward. With every wave, the sense of evil recedes from me. Finally, it is not touching me anymore. I watch as it disappears.

The following morning, I was sitting cross-legged on the floor. Next to me was a breakfast of ham and eggs. I couldn't eat it. Miss Camilla was sitting in the same club chair, looking at me. She was wearing a yellow caftan, the first time I'd seen her in that.

"So, this is my new home," I said.

"Yes, for now. Did you sleep at all?"

"Only a little," I said.

I clutched my head. "I have to figure out what to do about…

everything."

She nodded. "Can I ask something?"

"What?"

Miss Camilla leaned forward. "Now, I'm not asking—well, okay, maybe I am. Just where have you *been* for the last month?"

I sighed and leaned back on the sofa, shutting my eyes and holding my arms over my head. Then I took a deep breath and told her my whole story, starting with the birthday and proceeding through everything.

When I finished, she was looking at me with new eyes. "So, you're one of those people."

"What people?"

"You're touched."

"I don't know about that, but I can hear that girl Grace speaking to me. That's why I have to do something—wake her up, get her out. She's the key to everything."

"I used to work in that hospital," said Miss Camilla.

That pricked my attention. "What did you do?"

"I was a nurse. I was on the staff for more than twenty years."

I felt every nerve in my body sharpen. "Could you get her out of there?"

"What do you mean? Would we check her out?"

"No," I said, "I mean steal her. She's in a coma."

Miss Camilla blanched at that, sinking back a little farther in her chair. "I suppose so. I only retired last year, and I don't think they would've changed procedures yet."

"How could we do it?"

She leaned forward and put her fingertips together. I'd never seen her so purposeful. "Well, you'd start by visiting when the nurses are distracted, which is when they're changing shifts."

"Would it be easy to do?"

"Oh my goodness, yes. As long as a patient isn't coding,

nurses are always chatting."

As we put together the seeds of a plan, I began to feel excited. I was taking charge of the mystery that my life had become.

Sure that every car behind me was a cop car, I returned to the hospital the next day. First, I went to see Cy.

He was sitting up in bed. Before him was a big tray of institutional-style grub, crusty meatloaf and mushy peas, and he was shoveling the food into his mouth as fast as he could. It appeared that he had turned the corner, health-wise, certainly appetite-wise.

He waved at me with his fork. "How, paleface. Me Cy." Then he grinned hugely.

I was astonished. He'd never cracked a joke like that before. The change in the old man's behavior was remarkable, and it was apparent that his experience with the glowing light in the cavern was liberating. I was happy for him, almost to the point of forgetting the sorrow of the loss of my family, almost.

"You almost starved yourself to death," I said.

"It was worth it," he said, chewing. "The stuff I learned ... I got the Proof."

He was about to explain more when a young, portly doctor came into his room. In his hand was a tablet, which was apparently how they handled charts here. I watched his finger scroll through the pages. "Looking better, Mr. Kennedy," he said in a Middle Eastern accent, "looking better."

"Thank you," said Cy.

I glanced at the old man. "Your last name is *Kennedy*?"

"Yeah."

I laughed, a forced, nervous laugh, I realized, as laughing

for real seemed out of the question with what had happened to my family. "You could have given me a hundred guesses, I never would've thought *Kennedy*."

He shrugged his shoulders. "Our last name used to be Tailfeather. My dad got tired of being teased so he changed it to Kennedy. I decided to leave it the same to honor my father."

The doctor, who had been listening to our exchange with a smile on his face, put down the tablet. "We will keep you under observation for a couple more days and then release you if everything checks out."

"Thanks," Cy said.

"Make sure you don't eat too much," he warned.

He walked out of the room. I waited until the door closed, then turned to Cy. "You're welcome for saving your life." I smiled.

"Did I forget to thank you?" He caught my eye. "So, did you see if she was out of her coma yet?"

"Who?"

"Grace."

My jaw dropped. "How did you know that she was here?"

"Because I felt it when you touched her in her room two days ago. It was like throwing a switch. Any C.A. 2 could feel it. You were connected in the spirit realm, and that touch connected you in this one. Besides, she and I have some prior connection, you know."

"What? How?"

"Another time. Go to her."

"I came here to steal her," I admitted. "I have a plan and even a helper. Grace has been calling me for weeks."

"She has a very strong presence," he said. "The energy that surrounds her is phenomenal." He motioned to the third floor. "I can feel it from here. But I think she knows the power doesn't come from her. She is just the caretaker of that power. As it was given to her, she freely gives it to others."

That was a lot to chew on, so I pulled the conversation back to the mundane. "I'm using your truck," I said, "so when they discharge you you'll have to find your own ride."

"They said that won't happen for a few more days. You want to show me where Grace is?"

"You feel strong enough to walk?"

"Maybe, but I might need a hand."

I held out an elbow. Cy pulled himself very slowly out of bed. Together we went out into the hall and upstairs to the third floor. We made our way down the mostly empty corridor toward Grace's room. The door to her room was closed, but through the window in the door I could see that she was still lying in bed. Someone had changed her clothing and brushed her hair.

Cy looked pained. "I hope your plan works. From what I overheard the nurses saying, there was a Jane Doe in a coma on the third floor who's going to be institutionalized this weekend if her family can't be located. Are there any other unidentified girls in a coma up here?"

"I'm guessing not," I said.

"Then this is your only shot."

We both looked at her one more time. I put one hand on the narrow window in the door.

You're here.

I closed my eyes. *I'm going to rescue you.*

Hurry.

It's almost ready.

The communication ended. I pulled myself away from the door and noticed Cy looking at me. "So what did she say?"

"She's waiting for me to rescue her."

"It sounds like a fairy tale."

I could see why he would say that, except that the princess was in a coma and speaking to me telepathically.

"It kind of is—and you're going to help."

He grinned. "I can't wait to hear how. Just make sure I don't have to run anywhere."

"You won't."

Together, we shuffled back downstairs to his room.

That night, I sneaked into my home again—no more cop cars to watch out for—and entered my father's workshop. It was a creepy feeling, moving around among all of his bits and pieces of projects, the odds and ends of an endlessly inventive mind. I still could not believe that he was gone. I expected him to walk in, to grin at me, to get to work on his toys. But it was just beginning to sink it that he would not be back, ever, nor would my mother and brother, and something in me wanted to die, too.

I steadied myself, blinked, got my bearings again.

Over to the left I saw the helmets. I was shocked. Miss Camilla was right. My father had been trying to build helmets almost exactly the way that I had described them—a pair of antennae, a band of circuitry above the brow. It nearly made me cry. He believed in me! He had taken what most fathers would have dismissed as his kid's wacky dream, and he ran with it and made it a reality. I always knew that I had scored by having him as a father; now I knew it more than ever with his passing, and with his gift to me, even in death.

But I did not come for the helmets. I was here to look for ways to help transport Grace to a new location. Breaking someone out of a hospital who was in a coma carried a whole host of weird problems that needed to be addressed. For one, we needed a wheelchair, and Miss Camilla had an extra one in her home, something her mother had used.

I pondered. Grace would need some head support when she was in the upright position. So I cut a piece of plywood in the shape of someone's back and head. I then connected it to the wheelchair, along with a pillow, the U-shaped type that are used to support your head when you fly in an airplane. But I still needed to find a way to secure her to the chair. I spotted a roll of duct tape on the workbench. Then I stopped myself—that would be too sticky, too noisy, too painful, too…icky. There had to be something else around here. Looking through the cabinets and shelves, I found four large rolls of Velcro. Two were self-adhesive and two could be sewn on. That would do perfectly.

When I was finished, I remembered one more thing. I went over to my father's electrician's tool chest and rummaged around until I found an insulated wire crimper. It was to cut Grace's monitors in case Miss Camilla could not disable them.

Now, if Miss Camilla had done her job with the mannequin, everything should ready.

Miss Camilla *had* done her job, and when we arrived at the hospital the next evening, I drove Cy's truck into a parking spot far from the entrance, well out of view. I pulled the wheelchair from the back bed and opened it. Miss Camilla assembled the mannequin, which we'd dressed in a heavy shawl that covered its face.

Miss Camilla took a final look and adjusted the mannequin's limbs. "It's more like this. Old people in wheelchairs don't have the strength to keep their wrists on their lap."

"Are we ready?" I asked.

"Absolutely."

We pushed the fake person in the wheelchair into the hospital. A greeter asked if we were checking in. "No," said Miss Camilla, "we're visiting a patient. Is that you, Lucy?"

The greeter broke out into a big smile. "Miss Camilla! We sure do miss you around here!"

It went on like that as we moved through the hospital, strangers in scrubs stopping to chat with their former coworker. Miss Camilla had apparently been very popular.

We entered Cy's floor and spotted a nurse at her station. Not the same nurse I had spoken to before, which I was good with, but she recognized Miss Camilla right away.

Well, well! Don't you look good, baby!"

They embraced.

"I'm just getting off," said the nurse. "You caught me at a bad time."

"We're here visiting Cy. This is Cy's mother, but she doesn't like to talk, so we're just gonna keep on going."

"Welcome, Mrs. Kennedy," said the nurse loudly.

I bent over and in a loud voice said, "The nurse says hello, Mrs. Kennedy." I put my ear down by her mouth, pretended to listen, then shook my head. "She has some laryngitis."

Without any hesitation, we moved down the hall. The nurse glanced at us now and then but was too busy packing up to really pay much attention. Miss Camilla pretended to offer the mannequin a drink of water. It looked just real enough to fool anybody who was watching.

When we got down to Cy's room, he was waiting for us on the bed. "I'd love to meet my mother," he said.

"Here she is." I rapped the mannequin on the head with my knuckles. He laughed. "And this is Miss Camilla. She's helping me."

"Pleasure," he said.

"Okay, let's get up to the third floor. Ready for a leisurely stroll?"

"You bet."

The three of us pushed the wheelchair into the hallway, into the elevator, and rode it to the third floor.

"She doesn't talk much, does she," said Cy.

"Like mother, like son," I said. "You even forgot to tell me you were going to try to enter the cave."

We went out into the hallway. It was deserted at this time of night.

I wheeled the mannequin into Grace's room and shut the door. "Quickly now," I said.

Miss Camilla disabled and disconnected the monitoring equipment as Cy and I lifted the mannequin out of the chair and moved to the bed. Grace was stretched out there, same as before. As we lifted her body, she felt oddly light—as though there was something inside of her that was definitely ethereal.

We gently propped Grace in the chair. I used the U-shaped pillow and Velcro to secure her. Then we took the clothing off the mannequin and dressed her in it. Time was ticking by. We needed to get back out in the hallway as soon as possible.

Then we were finished. As long as no one looked too closely, she could pass for Grandma Kennedy.

Doubling our speed, we put the mannequin in the bed, covered it, turned its face away from the door, and arranged everything to look like an actual person was lying there. Our hopes were that we would be long gone before anyone noticed—and that they would not associate us with Grace's disappearance. As long as nobody saw us go in to or out of her room, we should be good. The camera view was obscured at both entrances to the rooms, so we knew we had a fighting chance.

We rolled Grace into the hallway and back toward the nurse's station and the elevators. The nurse would get a full-on view of our kidnapping victim as we approached, so I obscured Grandma Kennedy's face by bending over and acting like she was saying something to me.

We piled into the elevator, and it seemed like forever until the doors closed. The descent in the elevator felt like it took an hour. As soon as the doors opened to the second floor, Cy got off.

I waved at him, then jabbed the button marked L. The elevator descended again, and when the doors opened this time, I pushed Grace across the lobby floor and out the front door.

"Slow down, William—you're going to hurt her," said Miss Camilla.

I was starting to panic, since part of me knew that we could be easily arrested for this crime. Without delay, we rolled across the parking lot to the truck. We opened the back gate and lifted Grace from the wheelchair and laid her in the bed in the back. We secured her head and then placed the cinder blocks along her body so she wouldn't roll. We covered her with blankets, tucking them carefully around her body. She would be invisible to passing cars, though trucks could look down and see her. I folded the wheelchair and put it at her feet.

Then I got behind the steering wheel and started the truck and drove the forty-five minutes in silence back to the neighborhood. Miss Camilla kept an eye on the girl in the back.

We arrived in our neighborhood, my stomach an absolute wreck. As usual, I parked several blocks away. We reassembled the wheelchair and put Grace in it, and then I left Miss Camilla to wheel her around the block. I would cut through the backyards under cover of night.

It worked perfectly. Twenty minutes later, I sneaked in the back gate and was in the basement. Miss Camilla was tending to Grace, who was stretched out on the sofa.

You're safe now, I communicated to her.

Grace responded. *Thank you.*

For the rest of the evening, I sat with Grace. She was like a princess, to look at her, with that long hair and upturned nose. How could someone in a coma appear so perfect?

She was quite agitated, though, and her thoughts were not as smooth as before. I couldn't quite understand her communication. It was apparent that in telepathic discussion, if one of the participants is unsettled, it is very difficult to make a coherent connection.

Finally, her thoughts began to smooth out and I could make sense of them. *He wants me dead, and he is nearby.*

Who? I asked.

Him.

I don't understand.

You will. Soon.

Can I help you wake up?

No. I want to stay in this hidden state. As long as my consciousness is not exposed to the world he cannot find me.

What does he want from you? I asked.

He has been trying to destroy me since before I was even born.

I thought about that one for a while. These sort of reveals told me that the nature of evil was longer, deeper and more entrenched than humans would like to admit. That there has always been evil in this world, always will be evil in this world, and that our task is to simply fight it—continually, eternally.

William, you must be careful. If he gets too close to you, he will know I have communicated with you. My energy leaves a trail and anybody that stays in close contact with me is in danger.

I let go of Grace's hand and stepped away from the sofa. I wanted to know more, but it now became very clear why she was trying to hide things from me. Part of me questioned my own sanity, whether she truly was in danger—or if she was just a girl in a coma, and I was a lunatic, and the events of the recent past as I remembered them where just the false reality of a madman.

All I knew is that I couldn't figure out my next step until she woke up.

CHAPTER FOURTEEN

I t was still too dangerous for me to park the car or be seen in front of my family's house, but with the police presence gone, it was probably okay for me to stick my head slightly out of my shell.

And the only person who I trusted enough to contact was Arthur.

I knew that he had his hip-hop dance class on Thursdays. I spent a lot of time making fun of his silly moves. Still, I'd never taken dance classes, so I had to admire his gumption. And girls were always surprised when this monkey-armed guy started grinding away in the middle of a school dance.

So I took the truck on Thursday night and parked it outside the dance studio, which was at the end of a strip mall. I waited behind the wheel with my sunglasses and baseball cap on, feeling like a celebrity trying to avoid the paparazzi, which must be better than what I was hiding from.

At last he came out of the dance studio, dressed in black

sweatpants. Smiling, I rolled down the window and made a short, low whistle.

Arthur looked over. It took a couple of seconds, but he recognized me. He turned and ran up to the truck.

"Dude!" he said. "Is it you?"

"In the flesh," I said.

"I honestly thought you were dead," he said. Then his face fell. "You know about…"

I cut him off. "Yeah, yeah. Get in. I need your help."

He slid into the passenger seat and stared at me as though I were a phantom. It made me feel a little special, as though I'd survived something that other people hadn't. Which I had, of course.

"They think you did it," he said.

"I know. That's why I'm like this. You don't think I did, right?"

"Seriously? You can't even step on an ant."

I put the truck in gear and pulled out onto the road. "Where are we going?" Arthur said, wiping his forehead on his sleeve.

"Nowhere. I just have a few things to tell you."

"Like where you've been?" His eyes were popping out of his skull.

It took almost fifteen minutes to tell him everything. When I finished, Arthur sat in silence.

"Whoa," he finally said. "Either you've been trippin' on some bad stuff, or you're crazy, or we both are."

"I know. So, I'm approaching you for one reason."

"What's that?"

I looked at him. "I need help finishing the helmets."

His eyes flashed. "Count me in."

✧✧✧

Later that night, I sat on my father's workbench, cradling one helmet in my arm. Next to me, Arthur was studying the circuitry on the helmet.

"Your dad was really creative," he said.

"What do you mean?"

"Look at this." He pointed out a jumble of wires. "I never would've thought to arrange it like that." He looked up at me, but I had no idea what he was referring to. "What is the purpose of these things?"

"I told you, somebody showed them to me in a vision."

Arthur stared at me, uncomprehendingly, as though a dog had just walked by on its rear legs, smoking a cigar, which would be appropriate here. "You can't be serious."

"And think about this—I feel like it was from some advanced civilization or space brother I don't know."

"Whoa," he said.

"So this is real, and I think that these helmets will be the things that can get me in touch with others in the spirit realm."

"The other side," he said. Then he whoo-whooed like a ghost.

"Exactly. But it's different than you think."

"Why?"

"Sometimes you're just a C.A. 1, but some people are C.A. 2, and a few people are C.A. 3, except the ones that go evil, and they get dropped to C.A. 0…"

Arthur's mouth had dropped open. He held up a hand, stopping me mid-sentence. "William, could I just work on the helmet? I am already confused enough, dude."

I stopped talking. If he wasn't ready to swallow this much information yet, I wouldn't force-feed it to him.

We blacked out the windows and put towels along the cracks at the edges of the garage door to block the light.

I watched Arthur get going on the helmet. As his hands

worked on the circuitry, he said, "So I was trying to understand how someone could speak with the spiritual realm using modern technology."

"What did you do?"

"I went on YouTube and learned about all the paranormal technology. Those devices don't use anything too weird. It gave me a lot of ideas." He went on to explain exactly how paranormal science will someday be viewed as an extension of regular science.

Then he pulled out my father's soldering iron and put on my father's protective mask. I turned around, partly to protect my eyes, but also because they were misting up. Every day now, flashes of anger and sadness and grief came over me, and I would cry or just check out. I hadn't even gone upstairs into my parents' bedroom. I couldn't bring myself to do it.

I wiped the tears and stood by and waited to assist Arthur.

Four hours later, Arthur displayed the helmets for my inspection. They seemed to be finished. "Remember," he said, "this is just my best guess."

Tucking them underneath our arms, we left the garage workshop and crept across the street under cover of night.

I wondered how much longer I was going to have to skulk around like a thief. This event, this awakening of mine, should have had me giddy with happiness, but the loss of my family and the horrible thought of going to prison weighed on me like nothing I'd known.

We ran into the basement through the back door. Grace was lying on the mattress on the floor, the same mattress that we'd used in Cy's truck, since Miss Camilla and I had decided that it was too dangerous to place her on the sofa, because she could roll off and hurt herself.

"Grace, Arthur. Arthur, Grace," I said.

"She's beautiful."

"She's out of your league," I cautioned. "She's a special life form."

"That's what they all tell me. So if you've spoken with her telepathically before, why don't you just keep doing that?"

"Because she always comes to me. I don't seem good at the other way around. And it can be a little weird, kind of garbled sometimes. I want to be able to start the conversation, and I want to make it clear. Now help me."

We put one helmet on her head, then the second one on mine. Arthur adjusted some of the wiring on mine. "Ready to go." He'd installed an on-off button on the right side of each helmet. "I'll push hers, you push yours."

"One, two, three," I said.

We pushed the buttons simultaneously. I spoke in my mind and waited for something—a light, a buzz, a sense of clarity, a voice.

Nothing.

"It's not working," I said.

Arthur tried a few more configurations over the next two hours. Miss Camilla even came down to offer her input. The results were the same. I took the helmet off my head and looked despondent.

"I did my best," said Arthur, removing the one from Grace's head and setting it on the floor next to mine. "Sorry, man. This is above my pay grade."

"There must be something else about these helmets that we don't know," I said.

Miss Camilla shouted down the stairs, her voice tense. "William, you have to hide yourself! We got company."

I ran to the foot of the stairs and looked up. She was distraught. "Who is it?"

"The police chief," she said.

✧✧✧

The Chief. Julia's father. I felt panic rising inside of me. Fortunately, Miss Camilla and I had already formulated a plan for this—and it involved a long piece of hollow metal that was standing in the basement.

The water heater. It was lying horizontally in the far corner, in the unfinished portion of the basement, next to the sump pump. The water heater had broken less than two weeks ago, and when she'd bought a new one, Miss Camilla insisted on keeping the old one. She was a packrat like that, I had learned. Nothing ever escaped her. I guessed that she might've had a lot taken away from her in the past.

"Crap," said Arthur.

"You're in no danger," I said. "You're not wanted by the police, but the two of us are. Help me load Grace into the heater."

He looked over at the thing. "There?"

"She fits. We already did a trial run the other day. Hurry."

We picked her up and loaded her feet first into the heater. Then we made sure the open end was facing away from the stairwell.

"What about you?" he said.

"It's cheesy, but I'm hiding in the closet."

Again, this was part of the plan. There was a large closet near the stairs, with a false door inside it. Miss Camilla said she'd had the house for years before she had found it, that maybe someone had stashed money in there or something.

I could hear the man's voice upstairs, coming closer. I went over and opened the door. Inside were all of Miss Camilla's caftans. I pushed through them, found the secret door, and slipped inside.

"Okay," I whispered to Arthur.

"Okay," Arthur echoed, and I heard the closet door close.

I was surrounded by complete darkness. I listened for the conversation upstairs, which was now quite muffled and indistinct, but when I focused I could make it out.

"May I look around down there?" the chief's voice said.

Miss Camilla responded, "My young friend is down there, working on a project. I'd rather not disturb him."

"Your young friend, eh? His name wouldn't be William, would it?"

"You told me who you're looking for. Of course that isn't him. That's Arthur."

That explanation apparently was not sufficient to satisfy the chief of police. "We can do this one of two ways. The first way is for me to look around freely inside the house, disturbing things as little as possible. The second is to inconvenience me by forcing me to go to the courthouse and get a search warrant. Which would make a frustrated individual even more frustrated."

"I don't know what you mean," said Miss Camilla. She was playing dumb.

"The detectives that will enforce the search warrant may not be as careful looking around," he said.

"So they're going to leave my home in a shambles."

"Possibly."

"You win, tough guy. Help yourself."

The hair on my arms stood up. I was safely hidden, but to say that I was alarmed was an understatement.

I heard the police chief's boots clack on the floor above my head. I pictured him strutting around like the big rooster in the henhouse, but then I heard his footsteps coming down the steps, reaching the basement, pausing near me. I could feel his presence, something I was getting better at as I grew into being a C.A 3. I held my breath and shut my eyes, not daring to twitch a single muscle fiber.

"Good evening, son," he said.

"Hi," I heard Arthur respond. His voice sounded quavery.

"What's your name?"

"Arthur."

"Last name?"

"Chernow."

"What're you doing here?"

"Miss Camilla asked me to build some experimental helmets."

"For what?"

"Telepathic discussions."

"What discussions?"

I heard Miss Camilla coming down the steps, walking over beside the police chief. "I have a passion for the spiritual realm, officer. Do you have any experiences with the other side? Those who once lived among us, who still do, but we can't see them?"

The chief was moving around the room, no doubt poking his fat nose in everything.

"I saw that old movie *Ghost*," he said. "It was stupid. Oh, and I saw *Ghostbusters*." To Arthur, "Have you spoken with William recently?"

"No," he lied.

"Are you positive?"

"Yes sir."

"You're across the street from his family's house."

"I know."

"And he's your buddy."

"Was my buddy."

"Was your buddy? You mean he's dead?"

"Don't know what or where he is. But haven't seen him

lately, so…"

"You have no idea where he might've gone?"

"No sir. Have you asked your daughter? She would know better than me."

I heard the police chief grunt. Then fingers rapped on the closet, mere inches from my face. "What's in here?"

"Some old clothing," Miss Camilla said. "See for yourself if you like."

"Hmm," he said. I could see him, in my mind's eye, or in my C.A. 3 eye.

I heard the door open, then the rustling of clothing and the scrape of hangers. Then he knocked—right on the wood, not an inch from my head! I flinched and inhaled sharply, but luckily I didn't bump anything or stumble backward. Man! He was *right there*. I was about to get busted and spend my life in prison—after this guy beat me to a bloody pulp with a nightstick.

"Can I show you the upstairs now?" said Miss Camilla.

"Yes, ma'am."

I heard the closet door close and their footsteps go up the stairs and echo through the rest of the house, and I caught a breath. A few minutes later, the front door slammed.

Arthur opened the closet door. "That was a close one, man. I think I peed my shorts a little."

"I told you to wait ten minutes, Arthur!" I said. "In case he doubles back."

"Oh, yeah!"

Arthur closed the door again, and I realized that I was the one who needed a bathroom.

❖❖❖

Later that night, after Arthur had left, I sat on the sofa looking at Grace. We'd returned her to the mattress and cleaned the bits of rust from the water heater out of her hair.

Then she found me again.

Kiss me.

I felt myself stiffen. That was asking a lot. *You're in a coma.*

I need to know that you love me.

I didn't know what to say to that. There were a thousand words in my mind all at once. Instead, I crossed the room and sat next to her on the floor and put my hand awkwardly upon hers.

William.

What?

I love you.

I felt my pulse quicken. *Okay.*

You're in my mind, but I want you to feel my body.

Are you sure?

Yes.

Cautiously, my hands began to rove over the contours of her body. I felt the softness of her neck, the flat plain of her stomach, the swell of her hips. It seemed wrong, considering that she was unconscious, but she wasn't, not really, and she was telling me to do it.

Now kiss me.

Carefully positioning myself, I slowly lowered my head until my lips touched hers.

Grace's eyes opened.

I yelped and scrambled backward. Her eyes followed me as I stumbled backward against the wall. It was like Sleeping freaking Beauty.

"You're ... you're awake," I stammered.

Her eyes took in the room. Her mouth opened slightly, and her tongue wetted her lips. Then she spoke, in a voice that sounded surprisingly young for such a old soul, her wisdom transcended the apparent age of the body she occupied.

"He … will find me now."

"Who?"

She didn't answer. "Can you … help me up?"

I rushed back to her, slipped my arms beneath her body, and helped her to a sitting position.

For the next two days, with my help, Grace slowly came back to her body. It was an amazing thing to watch. She looked like the Tin Man in the *Wizard of Oz*, her first movements stiff and restricted. Then, almost miraculously, she would somehow channel the energy that existed around her to do its task. With each increase of range of motion, she was extremely thankful, to Miss Camilla and me. Miss Camilla had taken over the task of feeding and physical therapy.

By the end of her second day, Grace could sit up without assistance and even stand, albeit wobbly.

"Who is coming for you?" I said.

"Him."

"Who is 'him'?"

She wouldn't look at me. "I don't like to say his name, William. But he is more evil than you can imagine. All evil. He is here to oppose us, destroy us, and take everyone and everything with him."

Some evil, other-worldly bastard is after us and, it sounded like, out to … destroy … what? Civilization? Bad news, worse news. It just kept coming.

"Have you met him?"

Grace nodded.

"How far away is he?"

"Not far. He's going to find me soon."

"How soon?"

"Days."

Days? Did she expect me to help? I was a C.A 3, apparently, but I felt like a novice, and I sure as hell didn't feel up to taking down "pure evil."

We both grew quiet and sat there a while.

Then I turned my attention to Grace, someone I had known, yet never met, someone new to me, yet someone I felt I loved, someone new to me, yet familiar.

I grew bolder. "Grace, ever since my birthday last month, nothing has been the same for me. I'm taking care of you because you called me to find you. And if we have days before this person is going to find you, you need to tell me everything."

Her eyes found mine. "Okay, William. I will tell you everything. But help me outside. I want to see the stars. It's been so long."

I helped her to her uncertain feet, and we went out the rear entrance of the basement and emerged in Miss Camilla's backyard. A thick wall of bushes bordered the yard, so nobody could see us.

I found a pair of outdoor chairs, unfolded them, and positioned them opposite one another in the grass. Then I seated Grace in one of them and threw a blanket over her shoulders. I sat in the other chair.

"Now," I said, "tell me why you were calling for me."

"Because you are the only one who can help us."

I sincerely doubted that, but Cy had told me I was a C.A. 3. I decided to start acting like one. "What do you need from me?"

"We have to stop him."

"Who is *him*?"

She looked up at the stars for a long moment, as though searching for something. When her voice came out, it was like a whisper.

"Roivas."

Roivas. I said the name to myself. It was strange, not unlike most things in my life these days.

"He goes by many names," she continued. "He is continually reborn. But to me, he is just Roland."

"Why do you know him as Roland?"

As her answer came out, it looked like it physically pained her. "Because he is my brother."

That stopped me in my tracks. "He's your *brother*?"

"He is very powerful, both in this world and the spirit realm. In this world, he senses people who have been given power. And he tries to destroy them before they can oppose him."

I pointed across the street toward my house. "Could he have been the one who killed my family?"

Her eyes found mine, and the sadness in them told me that it was true. I stood up from my chair and paced through the grass, my hands clenching my hair. Thinking about how they must have died. I wasn't a coward, but I was no superhero, either, and I did not want to die like that.

"I don't want anything to do with this," I said. "My family is dead because of this guy. I say we let the police handle him..."

Grace shook her head sadly. "He is beyond the police. This is beyond the power of most humans."

She must've seen the grief in my eyes.

"William, your parents and brother are not gone, not really."

Not gone? I had heard of the "afterlife" in church when I was a kid, but never put much stock in it.

Grace stood up and came over to me. She was wobbly but gaining strength by the hour, it seemed. "We can do this, but we can only do this together. You have a special gift that we need to develop. You felt it earlier."

"I did. With Julia's cousin."

"It was a shock, wasn't it?"

I nodded. She was touching on some of the stuff that I hadn't wanted to face, mostly because I did not know how to control it.

"You'll learn to control it," she said, sharing my thoughts again. "And we'll defeat him. Are you going to be with me?"

"Yes," I said, gathering my wits and my strength, if not my courage. "I want to stop him. I want to stop the person who killed my family and stop him from hurting others."

"In this terrestrial world, we must work this together," she said. "Roivas is too powerful for any one person to stand up to. If we can defeat him…"

She let the sentence go unfinished, and I suddenly knew what to say. "If we can defeat him, then we have a chance to reach Final Ignition. All of us."

Grace turned her head, perplexed. "What's that?"

I explained to her what I'd learned in the Hall of Knowledge, about the ten brothers. How three of our civilizations weren't altruistic enough, and once we learned to work together, and once we reached ten billion, we could reach ignition.

As I described it, the light of recognition dawned in Grace's eyes. "I remember now. That's our mission, isn't it?"

I nodded.

"Can you take me to this Hall of Knowledge?"

Doing that made sense to me. Going back to the reservation was safer than remaining here, or at least it would be freer. Cy may or may not have been released from the hospital. At least, he hadn't tried to contact me.

"When do you want to leave?" I said.

"As soon as I'm strong enough."

That was a point. She could hardly be expected to go crawling through tunnels quite yet. I turned my chair to sit alongside hers. We took our seats and, as we looked up into the sky, I found Grace's hand and held it.

CHAPTER FIFTEEN

A day later, we determined that Grace was strong enough to leave. During the last twenty-four hours, she had grown healthy, like a wilting weed that had been watered. I phoned Arthur on Miss Camilla's house line.

"Yeah," he said.

"Are you interested in going on an adventure?" I said.

"To where?"

"I'm going back to the reservation. Grace is awake and she wants to see the Hall of Knowledge."

"Do you think I can get in? You said the tunnel was really small."

"Just those monkey arms."

"What?"

"Nothing. Honestly, no," I replied, "but I still need your help. Those helmets aren't finishing themselves."

"Yeah, I've been learning more about how the paranormal investigators are using these crazy tools. So, electrostatics is, like, my favorite field now."

"All right," I said, "I'll pick you up at noon."

"Um, William, maybe you've been gone too long, but I don't get out of lab until 2:30."

School. I'd forgotten about that. It was September again, and everybody I knew was back in classes. "All right, I'll pick you up from school at 2:30. Pack some clothes and a sleeping bag. Look for the old truck."

"If you want me to keep working on the helmets, be sure you bring all those tools from your dad's garage."

"Yup," I said.

We disconnected, and I turned to Grace. "We leave tomorrow at 2:30. Let's get ready."

The next afternoon, Miss Camilla gave us a going-away gift—a home-packed lunch. I unwrapped it and saw sandwiches, potato chips, pickles.

"I owe you my life, Miss Camilla," I said.

"Don't mention it, baby," she said. "I know you didn't trust me before, but now that's all changed. You needed support."

"I promise to come back and see you, but it's dangerous for us to be here."

She took me by the hand and gazed into my eyes. "You have to take care of yourself. You could be getting in over your head."

I squeezed her hand. "I don't have a choice."

We embraced, and Grace thanked her. Then we slipped out of the basement, hoodies over our heads, and hustled across the yards toward the truck. I'd have to drive, even though I had no license, but I knew that getting ticketed for that was the least of my worries.

Ten minutes later, I pulled the truck into the parking lot of my high school. I parked near the rear of the asphalted area, baseball cap and sunglasses pulled low over my face. Grace wasn't known here, so she sat next to me, face uncovered.

"So, Arthur is a good guy," I explained. "You can trust him with your life, and he would do anything for me. I mean, he made the helmets that I used to try to communicate with you."

"Where did you get that idea?" she said, smiling.

"They came to me in a dream or vision or something like that. Kind of weird. It was right after I saw this strange dude with cold eyes do this whacked-out wink. I think his name was Hunter."

Her mouth fell open. "You know him?"

"He came to me in a dream. Do you know him?"

She waved off the question and turned away. "We have enough going on right now. We can talk about it later."

I didn't have a chance to try getting more out of Grace because Arthur came walking up. He had a book bag in one hand and a duffle bag in the other. He threw both in the bed of the truck, opened the passenger door and got inside as she slid over.

"Arthur, this is Grace."

"We already met," he said, eyes wide as he took her in, "but you were unconscious, so you know, you probably don't remember."

I started the engine and headed back the way we came. "You can't go that way," said Arthur. "They're stopping anybody who doesn't follow the arrows now."

"But the arrows lead right in front of the school doors."

"Yeah, but if they stop you, you're screwed."

Frowning, I wheeled around and followed the arrows on the asphalt around the parking lot. We got stopped in a line of cars waiting to get out. Students poured around the car on their way out of school.

"Keep your head down," said Arthur.

"I am."

We inched forward. The main road was only a hundred feet ahead, but it was taking the cars forever to turn because of traffic. Suddenly a figure stepped in front of my hood. It took me a second to recognize her.

It was Julia.

She came around the truck, dressed all in black like some Ninja, maintaining laser eye contact with me with those huge brown eyes. I rolled down my window.

"Look…"

"What the hell are you doing? Seriously? I thought you were dead, too!"

"No, I had… some trouble."

"We need to talk…"

"I'm leaving town, right now."

"I want to know what happened to you!"

Her voice rose, almost to a shriek. This was the last thing I wanted—Julia making a scene. I had already noticed the security guard peering over at us, and with a quick glance I saw that he still was. I grabbed Julia's hand, yanked off my sunglasses with my other hand and smiled for the guard's sake, as I looked deep into her eyes.

"Julia, there's no time. Let me summarize. I discovered I have some special gift, and the people in the truck could help save human civilization. Sounds crazy? I know, but it's not. I'm not. Now, you need to decide. If you want to come with us, good. If you want to stay here, then you never saw me. Which is it? Please!"

She stared at me, her mouth opening and closing like a gasping fish.

"You have to make a decision *right now*," I said, nodding

toward the line of cars. "I'm out of here."

"I'm coming," she said.

"Then get in the other side. Arthur, slide over."

Julia came around to the passenger seat. A few seconds later, all four of us were squished into a single bench.

"Hi, Julia," said Arthur. "I can't believe you found us."

"It was your big butt that made me notice this truck," she said. "By the way, whose truck is this?"

"We'll answer all your questions on the drive," I said.

"I talked to your dad," said Arthur. "He's still looking for William."

"The whole world is looking for William," she said.

As we neared the exit lane to leave the school grounds, I managed to get my sunglasses on before we reached the security guard, who frowned as he stared into our truck. Julia waved and smiled, but as we passed, I saw him in the rearview mirror, peering at us.

I floored the accelerator and sped out of the parking lot.

The drive was incredibly tense, as we expected cops to surround us, guns out, at any minute. After taking a series of turns off the main roads, we found our way back to the highway.

We arrived at the cabin shortly before dusk. Everyone fell out of the truck and stretched their legs, and to my surprise a light turned on in the cabin. Cy came out onto the porch. He looked healthy and moved with more strength than before.

"I was waiting for you," he said.

I introduced all the others. He ran a hand through the back of his hair. "I don't know where all of you are going to sleep," he said.

"I brought my own bag," said Arthur.

"And William and I can share a bed," said Julia, glancing smugly at Grace.

"We'll figure this out," he said.

Later, in the cabin, we built a fire, and Cy warmed several cans of pork and beans in a cast-iron pot over the flames. As the five of us sat around the hearth feeling the warmth driving away the high-altitude nighttime chill, we started talking and explaining to Julia and maybe to ourselves.

"Grace, how do you know William?" asked Julia.

I sensed a girl wanting to size up the competition, so I played damage control.

"She's a Change Agent too," I said.

"But how did you meet?"

"She spoke to me telepathically because she was in a coma, and I rescued her. Then she woke up." I didn't mention what occurred when I had kissed her.

Julia's eyes grew alarmed. "No way."

"But what's the story of your life?" asked Julia, turning to Grace. "Like, how did you get this power?"

Grace finished her pork and beans, set the bowl on the floor, and wiped her mouth with a napkin. "Well, there's a lot that William doesn't even know yet. Are you ready to hear it?"

"Sure," I said.

"You were involved in a snap at a theater in Las Vegas. You, me and Jeremy. Remember?"

"No," I admitted, "I'm not there yet."

"Do you remember Jeremy?"

I shook my head.

"Do you remember what a snap is?"

"No."

"They're moments when members of our group inhabit someone else's body, sometimes just for a few minutes, sometimes for days. It happens for individuals after they're separated from their original parallax, they're original viewpoint as people."

"Is it like an out-of-body experience?" asked Arthur.

"Sort of," she said, "and William and I knew each other in a previous iteration, as we were part of the same group."

"I do *not* remember that," I said.

"The other members were Jeremy and... *Hunter.*"

Grace put extra sauce on that name, and suddenly it all made sense. "The guy who visited me in my dream," I said.

"Yes, and he's always looking out for himself. He is very cold and calculating in everything he does," she added. "He showed you the helmets because we're going to need them for something. Anyway, back to the snap."

"Yes, please," said Julia. I could see from her face just how amazed she was. And I was able to process it better, since it was all finally starting to sink into my thick melon.

"During the snap, there was a line of people that were waiting to enter the theater. A car jumped the curb and was mowing down pedestrians. Jeremy somehow recognized the people standing behind him and pushed them out of the way. He died in the process. Because choices made in snaps impact both the earthly realm and the spiritual realm, Jeremy died that day in both realms.

"What we did not know was that Jeremy and I were supposed to be twins on earth. My new mother was devastated. There were no longer two heartbeats growing inside of her. The decision was made by the doctors to allow her to go full-term to complete the development of me, the little girl. My new Earth family are spiritual people, and my father is the pastor of a church, so they prayed continually for a miracle. Beyond all possible odds, something incredible happened."

"What?" said Cy.

"Just before I was born, the medical team was able to pick up two heartbeats from inside the womb. They couldn't understand how that could be possible. Complications set in, and since I seemed to be a breech birth anyway, it was a very delicate situation. That's when my heart stopped beating. They decided to do an emergency C-section. As they pulled me out, to their surprise my new twin had his legs wrapped around my neck, trying to choke me. It took the medical team several minutes to get my heart and lungs working.

"My parents were amazed—it was two miracles in the same day. What was thought to be dead was now alive, and what was alive died and came back to life. Me and Roland."

"Better known as Roivas."

Cy spoke up. "We call him Little Horn."

Everyone looked at the old native. He was calmly eating his beans, listening to our conversation like it was the most normal thing in the world.

"Did you make that up?" asked Arthur.

"Of course not, idiot," Cy replied, "that's our traditional name for this creature. He comes back in various iterations, but he's always the same."

"Absolutely evil," said Grace.

"What did he do that was so bad?" said Julia.

"I think that he knew from birth that I would be the one who could reveal his true identity. Later, he was always doing things that were very evil and would blame me. He put a kitten through our family's meat grinder and said that I had done it. He ran over my baby rabbits with our lawnmower and blamed that on me, too. He almost killed our grandfather by knocking out the hydraulic jack that was holding up the car in the garage. It came down on Grandpa, almost crushed him, and he ended up having to have both legs amputated. Later Roland set our house on fire."

She paused. Cy and Arthur and I were speechless. "How many more stories like that do you want to hear?" she said. "'Cause I have a hundred more."

Cy made a gesture that said *enough*. "Do you feel very connected to him?"

"How can I not? Some of his evil essence trickled into my being. I have learned how to keep it at bay, but it allows him to have a connection with me."

Grace explained that she had experienced a breakdown. She too had reached her sixteenth birthday and ignition point nine months prior to me. Her tormented mind coupled with in-depth memories pushed her over the edge, and her family decided to institutionalize her. She was hysterical about Roivas trying to kill her and her family, and so they put her on a regimen of therapy and medication in the hopes of stabilizing her so-called mental condition.

After she had spent several months in the mental-health facility, questions began to arise whether she would ever be able to function in society again. She talked constantly about how Roivas was trying to harm her and prevent her from revealing his identity. The staff was beginning to characterize her as delusional with schizophrenic tendencies. Grace was coherent enough to realize that this treatment program wasn't going to lead anywhere.

"Plus I kept saying another name," she said.

"Whose?" I asked.

She looked at me. "Yours, William. I knew you were out there. Remember, we existed together, before our time in this realm."

I started to respond, but Cy cut in. "So Roivas is still alive right now?"

"First let me finish my story," she said. Grace continued describing the psych ward.

As I listened, I realized that I could have ended up in that kind of place. The people I had shared my story with were leery, but in the end they believed as best they could. I could see, though, that all these crazy thoughts and dreams and events might have led me over the edge, where I could have spent my life drugged up in some cold institution.

Inside the mental hospital, Grace wondered if they weren't right, if she was crazy. She had grown up being tormented by Roivas, and that place was making it all worse, not better, and she was not sure what was real. Then she gathered her wits and began to formulate a plan to escape. Every evening she was given medication, sedatives. The staff made her open her mouth to make sure that all the pills were gone. She became quite adept at locating and moving one pill underneath her tongue. After a week, she had collected seven pills.

The attendant who issued the medication every night always flirted with her. She never responded to his advances until that last week. He always carried a stainless-steel coffee cup with a plastic lid. The night of her escape, she slipped the medication into his coffee cup. An hour later, he was passed out in a chair. She took his keys and found her way to the locker room where staff changed. She rummaged through some lockers, found some street clothes, and quickly walked out.

"Three days later," she said, "I was outside that shopping mall. I had been drawn to it, and I saw you and Julia drive past and park in the lot. I watched you go into the sporting goods store. I could feel that you and I were close, that you were the Change Agent I was seeking. Then you had that burst of energy inside, and it was confirmed. So I followed you to the bus stop. I got on after you. I sat behind you and watched you. When you got off in the middle of nowhere, I slumped down so the driver couldn't see me, and when I popped up a few minutes later he nearly had a cow! I got off, sat out in the desert, and contacted this guy. I could sense him. He was a Change Agent."

She pointed at Cy.

I sat in shock, stupefied, slack-jawed. Then I turned to Cy. "You've met her before?"

The old Indian grinned. "She came to me in a vision, told me to drive out and pick you up."

She smiled. Cy smiled. I shook my head and wondered how many times the world was going to pull the wool over my eyes and then laugh at me.

"Why didn't you just talk to me when I got off the bus?" I asked.

"Looking back at it, I should have. But I was still unsure if you understood enough to help us or help yourself. And I knew I was close to the Hall. So I went to it."

"Yes," he said, "she helped us find the Hall of Knowledge."

I had grown utterly silent, realizing just how much I didn't know. How could I be a Change Agent? How could I affect change if the knowledge I had access to just came out in little drips and drabs? Was I an incompetent Change Agent, a failure who these others had put their misplaced trust in? Really, I wanted to go back to the way things were, back to being just a punk kid, stumbling around, clueless, griping about everything. This was my first lesson about being "careful what you wished for." It was something the older folks had said over and over again but this was the first time I understood. Not that I had wished for anything quite like what was happening now, but I sure thought I hated high school and my parents telling me what do and being bored. Now I would have given anything to have all of that back.

Arthur and Julia sat, rapt as Grace described how she'd followed her intuition to the cave, listening telepathically for anybody who might be giving her hints.

"I think the L.Es—the first people to reach final ignition— were helping me. They're always trying to help us reach final ignition."

Cy looked at her admiringly. "That's a true Change Agent right there, everybody. Messages from the L.E. Maybe that's who gave me the vision of the helmets?"

Grace blushed, then continued. Once she'd located the cave, she was able to identify the rock and push it away from the entrance to the tunnel. She had very minimal supplies with her, so her experience there wasn't nearly as thorough as mine. After locating the column of earth, she left a message for us.

"That was you?" Cy asked.

"The one thing that you didn't learn in the Hall of Knowledge was the fact that a Change Agent can imprint an image on the stone face. And if another civilization inputs information in the Hall of Knowledge, it will be transmitted to all ten worlds."

"I don't have that ability," I said.

"You will soon," said Cy.

I turned to Cy again. "And you knew about this all along?"

Cy nodded again. "You needed to discover some of these things for yourself." Then he addressed Grace again. "But you still haven't answered the question. What happened to Roivas?"

"I don't know," she said. "I was institutionalized."

"But he's your brother."

"My family stopped talking to me."

"Is he alive?"

"Yes. I have no doubt that he killed William's family. In

any case, he's so powerful that he'll come back, in any form, to hunt down the person or persons who know his identity." She paused. "That includes all of you."

Silence. None of us liked hearing that our knowledge might kill us.

"How did you end up in the hospital?" asked Arthur. "Did you just put yourself in a coma?"

"No," she said, "When I left the cave, I felt like I was being watched. I moved cautiously, and after a mile, I saw someone sitting on a large rock. It was an older man, and he motioned for me to come over. He said his name was Sonny."

William and Cy exchanged looks. "Sonny's a C.A. 2."

"He said he knew that I had been to the Hall of Knowledge. He told me that Little Horn was after me—that's the name he used, not Roivas—and that he wanted to know the location of the cave."

"Sonny is also a seer," said Cy.

"I could tell. He said he searches for evil, every morning and every night. He told me Little Horn was an evil manifestation from another realm, and that I was clearly a Change Agent."

"He thinks of such things right on his porch," said Cy, pointing across the valley.

"He told of the signs in the stars indicating the arrival of a powerful force. Then he told me to hide myself."

"So you thunked yourself on the head?" I asked. I hadn't meant for it to sound funny, but everybody laughed.

"No," she said. "After I focused and contacted Cy about picking you up, Sonny prepared a special potion for me. I swallowed it and went into a coma. Then he poked a few little holes in my leg and took me to the hospital and said that he'd found me out near the edge of the desert, that I was the victim of a snakebite."

"So that explains it," I said.

"And even during this comatose state," said Cy, "you found that you could communicate telepathically with William?"

"Yes. It was easy. We're connected."

Julia didn't like hearing that, and I didn't blame her, but hey, it's not like we were married. We all looked at one another for a moment. The cabin was starting to feel colder, the heat from the fire fading. Cy stood up and shoved more logs into the fire.

"So now what do we do? Your twin brother is Little Horn, my ancestors' traditional enemy, and we have to stop him. For the first time in history."

"I know what to do," I said. Their eyes turned toward me, and I felt the words come tumbling out, as though the plan were preordained. "Tomorrow, we go to the Hall of Knowledge. We look at the walls for final clues."

"There's a lot to decipher," said Cy.

"Maybe if we put all our heads together, we can learn something."

Arthur hadn't spoken in a while. I looked over and saw that he'd passed out with his head against the wall. Next to me, Julia looked scared and was probably wondering what in the world she was doing. Grace and I caught one another's eyes, and she shrugged.

"Let's talk more tomorrow."

CHAPTER SIXTEEN

That night, Julia and I shared the one thin mattress that I'd used the previous month. It was exciting to be sleeping with this girl for the first time, feeling her against my body, even if nothing sexual was going to happen. There were too many other people in the cabin.

She turned to me, and I felt her lips on mine. We lay like that for a while, just making out. Then she pulled back and looked at me.

"So what did you do with that girl?" she said.

"Nothing," I lied.

"You kissed her?"

"No."

"Swear it."

I gulped. "I swear it."

She softened in my arms. "Tell me you still like me," she said.

I didn't know how to reply without sounding like a total jerk. "Look, I've been so busy." Then something occurred to me. "Aren't your parents going to worry?"

"My dad is always worrying."

"He's looking for you. And he has a lot of resources available."

She sighed. "Can we not talk about him? I'm so over that right now."

"All right," I said.

We fell asleep in each other's arms, and I fell into a deep—and for this night—dreamless sleep.

Ten o'clock the next morning, I was coming out of the privy when Arthur came running up to me. "Dude, he's coming this way!"

"Who?"

"Julia's dad. The sheriff!"

I felt the panic, and followed him over to where Cy was sitting on the porch. Next to him was Sonny. I didn't realize that he could make it all the way over here.

"What's happening?"

"Sonny saw a pair of police cars coming up the long road to the reservation," said Cy. "They're about half an hour away."

"You can see that far?" said Sonny.

"I told you, he's a seer."

Sonny fixed an eye upon me. "I thought maybe you might want to know."

I looked at Julia, who was scared. "I think my dad thinks I'm in trouble," she said.

"No, he wants to find me," I said. I told her about the security guard outside the high school yesterday.

"This could be a short trip," I said. "Let's get to the cave, quickly, before he arrives."

Cy cleared his throat. "So you're going to leave me here to deal with this problem?"

I rubbed my face and shook my head. "No, Cy, I'm not. We have to face him when he arrives."

Next to us, Sonny had grown very still. His weathered hand flexed as it gripped the wooden railing.

"What's wrong?" said Cy.

His mouth opened and closed, and his eyes were fixed at some distant point on the horizon. I thought they looked a little cloudier too.

"He's coming," he said.

"I know, and we're making preparations for the sheriff."

Sonny's head turned, and his eyes slid toward mine. "No, not the police chief. *Him.*"

"Who?"

He looked at me. "Little Horn. Roivas.

After that it didn't take long for us to get moving. Arthur and Julia had bought some food at a supermarket on the way up the mountains, and now we hauled it out of the back of the truck and packed it as quickly as possible into duffle bags.

We weren't racing to outrun the police. We were racing to outrun Little Horn (as Sonny called him) or Roivas (as others called him) or Roland (as Grace called him). I decided not to call him anything. I didn't want him to exist, period.

Cy was putting together his own pack in the kitchen. I went up to him. He wasn't very expressive, but I could see the worry in the creases in his face.

"Cy, have you ever seen Little Horn?" I asked.

"No."

"What do you know about him?"

His nose twitched. "I've only heard the stories my people pass down. I don't like to discuss them."

"Do we have any way of fighting him?"

His lip stiffened. "Not in this realm."

Now I felt the panic ripping through me. "So we just run?"

"He's still going to find us, because he's looking for you and Grace. But the Hall of Knowledge might provide some sanctuary. He might find his powers weakened there."

Ten minutes after that, the cabin was locked up, and the five of us were marching down the trail through the high-altitude pine forest toward the cliffs. I had a heavy pack on my back, as did Cy, while Arthur, Julia and Grace were carrying duffle bags.

"How do you think your dad found us?" I asked Julia.

"He's the sheriff," she said, rolling her eyes. "He has spies everywhere. I'm sure he's had security guards watching me at school for years."

Next to me, Grace moved silently over the bed of pine needles. She was tall, almost as tall as me, and she moved lightly like a deer. We fell behind the others, far enough so that we could talk privately. "Do you remember anything about your past iterations?" I asked.

"For the first couple of months after my sixteenth birthday," she said, "I only got a flash of a memory, here and there. Now there's more."

"Who were you?"

"I think one of them was in the court of Marie Antoinette," she said. "I remember seeing the wigs, and the way she acted like a child. And just recently I remembered watching her lose her head, and feeling bad, because nobody deserves to die like that."

I thought about my parents, and grew sad. Grace grew quiet. "What about you?"

"Nothing, not yet," I said.

"It'll come." She looked at me curiously. "We knew each other. And the others, too."

"Who?"

"You were at odds with Hunter. There are two others as well."

I didn't know what to do. "So we travel through time…"

"No time travel," she said. "We went through iterations together. It's different."

"Sorry—we went through *iterations* together."

"Yep."

"Which are past lives."

"And we snapped together, too. Don't forget that."

I tried to remember. "So that's when you inhabit someone else's body for a while."

"Yes—it's like sharing someone's personality. It teaches us empathy in a way that nobody else can experience, except maybe through books."

I thought about that. It seemed that more people should be doing these snaps, however strange it sounded to say.

It grew colder. Overhead, gray clouds had slid across the sky like the lid over a sarcophagus, sealing out the sunlight. I felt a chill beneath my clothing and wished Sonny had stayed with us, but he'd returned to his cabin.

Cy held up a hand and stopped walking, and we all stopped behind him. "He's near."

"Little Horn?" said Julia.

He nodded. "Everybody, quick now, to the rope."

We broke into awkward little runs. It was nearly impossible for me, given the heavy pack on my back. Arthur was heaving after less than a minute, owing to his weight. Cy did more of a straight-legged speed walk. Julia and Grace moved better than us, though.

At last we made it to the small plateau. The rope was still there, hanging over the edge of the cliff.

"First, give me your packs," said Cy.

We set them down. Cy picked the first one up and calmly threw it over the edge. We heard it hit the rock cliff below. Then he did the same until every bag had gone down.

Then Cy turned to Arthur, Grace and Julia and explained to them what they had to do. Arthur's face turned ashen as he looked down with horror. "I don't think I can do it."

"It's not as bad as it seems," I said. "It's mostly arm strength. Just tense your upper body as much as you can, keep it tensed, and go down in big bounces. If you go quickly, you can make it in less than ten seconds."

"You go first, William," said Cy.

I grabbed the rope and let myself down the cliff, making big exaggerated bounces against the rock face so they could see how to do it. I'd grown quite good at it over the many trips I'd made here. Lickety-split and I was down on the rock.

"Who's next?" I shouted up.

A few seconds later, I saw Julia come down. She was agile, and even with her slender arms she managed to descend as though it wasn't her first time. Her feet hit the rock next to me, and we were both standing at the mouth of the cave. "Nice job!" I said.

"Thank you," she said. "This place is cool!"

Grace came next, a little more hesitantly, her arms trembling. She even slipped down the rope a few feet near the end, but I caught her in my arms. Her eyes were shocked.

"Surprised that you made it?" I said.

"No, I just remembered ... something else."

"Something from the parallax?"

Grace nodded, so I said, "Tell me later."

Arthur went third, and he was the most difficult. I realized that his arm strength needed to be double all of ours—he weighed nearly twice as much as Julia. His descent down the rope was nearly vertical.

"Slower!" I shouted. "Push off with your feet!"

He managed to slow down his descent. I could see the effort on his reddened face. But then he lost it—his hands released the rope, and he dropped the last seven or eight feet to the rock. He landed on his side.

The three of us ran over to him. Arthur's face was grimacing in pain, his mouth open like a baby who was too hurt to cry.

Julia crouched next to him and tried to touch him. Arthur shouted no, and she jerked her hand away.

"Cy," I shouted up, "you'd better get down here."

Cy descended the rope, and soon the four of us had circled around my hurt friend. Cy rummaged through his bag and produced a small pack of ointment.

"It's an old traditional recipe," he explained, squeezing the green stuff in a small circle on his palm, "made of twelve different plants."

"If he broke his arm, I don't know if it's going to help," said Julia.

"It has special properties," Cy mumbled.

We all stepped aside as Cy approached our fallen friend, rubbing his hands together. I could smell the herbal oils in the ointment as they broke into the air.

"Lift up his shirt," said Cy.

"Arthur, we're going to lift up your shirt," I said. "Does it hurt too much?"

Arthur shook his head, grimacing.

"Then just cut it away," Cy said. "I need to reach the trunk of his body."

I opened a small pocketknife and slipped it between Arthur's skin and shirt. "Don't move," I said. Then I slit the fabric upward, from the bottom hem almost to his chin. The shirt fell open in two flaps.

Cy got down and rubbed the ointment onto Arthur's fleshy folds. I saw his face relax, as the skin returned to a normal color.

"Oh my gosh, that *hurt*," he finally said.

"Can you stand?" I said.

"I don't know. My chest is killing me on the side."

"I think he broke a rib or something," said Julia. "I don't think we should make him move."

Cy looked up at me. "He can't squeeze through the tunnel anyway, and I can't either. You three go on without us." He studied me. "You remember the symbols from a month ago?"

I reached into a bag and produced a sheaf of papers. "These are my original drawings."

"See if they've changed," he said. "If so, copy them down. But first let's drag him inside a little bit."

The four of us formed a human chair, hoisted Arthur, and carried him just inside the mouth of the cave. The first patters of rain hit the rock just as we set him down.

"We'll be back soon," I said to Arthur.

"Stay safe," said Cy.

I escorted Julia and Grace to the back of the cave, where the heavy rock had been rolled in front of the tunnel. The three of us pushed it out of the way.

A gust of damp air blew out of the tunnel. It carried the scent of fresh moss and almost smelled green.

"Oh my gosh," said Julia.

"That's pretty cool," added Grace. "It's like entering another world."

Julia bent down and looked into the darkness. "We have to crawl through that?"

"Yeah," I said, inspecting a cracked fingernail. "I've done it fifty times."

"How far does it go?"

"I don't know, maybe sixty or seventy yards. Here, look, this is our trolley. Let's put everything you want to bring inside."

I showed them the pan, and we spent the next few minutes filling it with lights, drawing supplies, water and other items. Then we finished, and I handed the two girls the extra headlamps that I had taken from my dad's garage. Julia and Grace strapped them on, then stood there, looking at me. I realized that they were trusting in my leadership.

"I'll go first, and you follow. One at a time. And listen to my instructions."

I switched on my headlamp; they did the same. I dropped to my knees and began crawling. I had to remember to slow down, and to announce everything that was coming up. After a minute, I called back to ask how they were doing.

"I do not like this," Julia answered.

"I'm okay," said Grace. "It's kind of like being born again."

Another minute passed, and we arrived at the tight spot. "Girls, this is the worst part. Here's what I want us to do—we're going to do a horizontal conga."

"That sounds sexual," said Julia.

"It's not," I said, wishing it were.

I instructed them to hold onto the feet of the person in front of them, and that we were going to worm our way through a tunnel only slightly bigger than ourselves. I felt Julia grab onto my ankles.

"Go," I said.

We began to move in awkward ripples. I put a little too much effort, because I hit my head on the low ceiling. I groaned.

I heard Julia's voice. "What's wrong? I'm freaking out, we're going to get stuck, it's so small, I can't even…"

"Nothing's wrong," I answered, trying to keep her from panicking. "Faster now, let's get through this before we get claustrophobia."

We moved in rippling waves, making our way as a single chain through the tightest spot of the entire tunnel. "Keep it up," I said, breathing hard. "We're almost out of this."

I heard Julia crying, and Grace didn't say anything at all. I steeled myself and willed us to keep moving forward.

At last, we broke out of the tight spot, and I turned and did my best to help the girls out. We all stood in awkward low crouches, trying to recover our breath.

"That was the worst thing I've ever done," said Julia.

"It gets easier to take," I said.

I swung my headlamp toward Grace. She was looking down the tunnel. I followed her gaze. The greenish glow was back.

"That reminds me of something," she said.

"It was here when I rescued Cy, and it went away. Let's see if we can sneak up on it."

I monkey-walked down the rest of the low tunnel, as was my custom, the two girls aping behind me. At last we arrived in the cave, and while the girls spun around marveling at the space with their headlamps, I turned around and hauled the trolley through the tunnel. When it arrived, I set up the small dome light and turned it on.

Instantly, the green haze disappeared. The walls were illuminated, and the symbols stood out in stark relief. Julia and Grace sucked in their breath.

"Whoa—that's beautiful!" said Julia. "Who made this?"

Grace looked around calmly. She was reflective. "The L.E.s. They're trying to help us."

I explained to Julia that these symbols were from ten brothers who represented ten civilizations, and that seven of the ten had reached final ignition.

"What is that?"

"When a population reached ten billion, and when it becomes charitable enough, it reaches final ignition."

"And the L.E.," added Grace, "was the first civilization."

She pointed to the first column on the walls. Then I noticed something odd.

"Wait a minute," I said, rummaging through the bag for the sheaf of drawings. I pulled it out and held the first one up against the first panel of the walls.

"Look," I said. "This is the drawing I did of this portion of the wall a month ago. Do you notice anything different?"

We all crowded around and studied the drawing.

"The symbols have changed," said Grace.

She was right—the symbols had changed in some areas, but they stayed the same in others. I already knew that they could do that—after all, Grace had communicated with me via the wall, back when she was in her coma. But I hadn't seen any changes this drastic.

"It seems as if the L.E. are trying to communicate with us," she said.

"What are they trying to say?" asked Julia.

Grace shook her head. "I don't know enough about this."

"Cy might figure it out," I said. "Let's show them to him and see what he thinks. I nominate you, Julia, as the official sketch artist."

She nodded and bounced on her heels. It was good that Julia had so much talent for this sort of thing, and for the next few minutes, I helped set up her materials. Grace adjusted the dome light as needed.

Then Julia got to work. I'd never seen her draw before, but she was good—her fingers gripped the pen just right, and she minimized her head movements so that her eyes just flicked back and forth.

Grace and I stood nearby, waiting. "Do you remember speaking to me through the wall?" I said.

"Of course."

"You said 'Find me.'" I pointed to the section where it appeared. "Look, now it's gone. This Hall of Knowledge is like a hall of mercurial graffiti."

She didn't laugh. "Actually, it's more like a website, where the messages you see depends upon the messages you've responded to in the past."

I walked over to the section of the wall where it had appeared. I looked for any trace of the words *Find me*. They were gone. Instead, in its place was a row of three images—a human skull, a circle of stones, and a small rectangle. I tilted my head and stared at them again.

That was a message, and it felt like it was intended for me.

Grace and I waited, now and then changing the light as Julia requested. I was surprised at how fast Julia could work.

Then I heard a distant voice, coming from the tunnel. I went over and crouched down. It was Cy.

"What is it?" I said.

"We've got company!"

I had a pretty good idea what that meant.

"The sheriff?" I called to Cy.

"Looks like it. And some of his guys!"

We've got company.

I knew this might happen, of course. We had used Cy's truck. But what to do now? My mind reeled.

I could just stay down there. But I doubted the sheriff would leave without me. And we could not stay in the cave for very long without provisions. Should I send up Julia? Would that satisfy him? No. It wouldn't. I didn't see any choice but to sacrifice myself, let the others work, and hopefully, find some way out of jail. Jail! The prospect of it made me shake.

I turned to Julia. "It's your old man."

"Dammit!"

"I've got to get up there. Get him away from here."

"Won't work. He won't go away without me. I need to turn myself in."

"You can't!"

"You guys can finish this without me."

"Should I come?" asked Grace.

"No, you help Julia," I said. "This is more important."

I got down on my hands and knees and scampered through the tunnel. I made it through the tight spot in record time. The panic was propelling me.

I emerged from the tunnel, dusted myself off, and walked out to the mouth of the cave. It was raining full on now, and the valley smelled green and alive.

Then I saw him.

Sheriff Winters.

Tough guy. Cop. Julia's father. He was standing before me, chatting with Cy. Another deputy stood behind him. Arthur sat on a rock nearby, a makeshift bandage around his torso, looking miserable.

The sheriff saw me, and a multitude of expressions passed over his face—contempt, surprise, sympathy, curiosity. I was struck by how changeable his face seemed to be.

I drew in a deep breath and strode forward. "Good afternoon, Sheriff."

"William Hawk?" he said.

"Yes?"

"I inform you that I am placing you under arrest for assault. And probably a few other things we can discuss later."

I decided to play dumb. "What did I do?"

"For one, the assault of a minor by the name of Dean Winters." He paused. "My nephew."

"This isn't possible," I said. "It was a complete misunderstanding..."

He cut me off with a hand. "I've seen the tape. You used some voodoo magic to assault that young man for the crime of speaking to his female cousin." He paused again. "My daughter."

I didn't say anything this time, just stood there, uneasy, my eyes glancing at the weapon in his holster. I wasn't sure what sort of legal power he had out here on the reservation.

"But that's peanuts, son. You're a suspect in a multiple homicide."

"I didn't kill my family."

"We shall see. Now the most important question, and you better tell me what I want to hear. Where is my daughter?"

"I don't know," I lied.

"Last chance, Bucko."

"I haven't seen your daughter for a month."

"High school security guard reported that she entered a vehicle whose description matches the one in the driveway of this man's cabin." He pointed at Cy.

"Coincidence," I shrugged. "High school security guards are all idiots."

He took a step forward and picked me up by the collar of my shirt and pushed me against the rock wall. I steeled myself and looked him in the eye.

His lips were clenched so tight that they grew white. "I will kill you with my own hands if you don't tell me where she's at."

The deputy took a step forward, as if to restrain the sheriff, then stopped, thought better of it, and returned to his position. Cy and Arthur watched sadly. Neither of them had anything to do with the event in the sporting-goods store; and of course neither of them were wanted for murder. Neither of them could effectively stand up to a sheriff.

"Then you better kill me."

"If something happened to her you can bet that I will," he said. He motioned to his deputy. "Place him under arrest."

The sheriff stepped away. The deputy removed the handcuffs from his belt and came over to me. "Anything you say may be used against you in a court of law. You have the right to consult an attorney before speaking to the police and to have an attorney present during questioning now or in the future. If you cannot afford an attorney, one will be appointed for you before any questioning if you wish."

He turned me around and snapped the handcuffs on my wrists. They felt cold and sharp against the sensitive skin of my wrists. Then he faced me forward again and put a hand on my neck.

"Wait," said Cy.

He stopped. I was turned around. The elderly Native American had stood up. "I know where your daughter is, but you have to promise me something."

"I don't negotiate," said the sheriff.

"Then just do me this favor. Let him go, and arrest me instead."

"For what?"

"The abduction of a minor. Your daughter, Julia."

"But you didn't abduct her," said the sheriff.

"Yes, I did," insisted Cy. "I admit to the crime."

I stepped forward. "No, Cy!"

The sheriff looked at the deputy as if to say, what do you think? They exchanged shrugs. The deputy reached behind me, fumbled for his keys, then unlocked my hands. Shocked that they were letting me go, I shook out my arms. Nearby, I saw Sheriff Winters click his handcuffs onto Cy.

Then the sheriff looked over. "Lock him up again. We're taking both of them."

The sheriff gave Arthur a terrific shove, and he went sprawling backward onto the ground. I felt the deputy's hand pushing me down to the ground too, and then his knee in my back, followed by the cold click of the steel on my wrists.

"It's okay, William, don't worry. I've had a good life. You haven't done anything wrong, except get carried away with a new power that you didn't know you had. That you didn't even know you *had*."

He was staring at me as he said that final sentence, and it dawned on me what he was trying to say. Cy wanted me to feel the same rage that I'd felt in the sporting goods store, and to use it—now.

I felt the power suddenly blossom inside of me.

"You *lied* to me!" I said.

"As you did to me," answered the sheriff calmly. "My daughter is here somewhere. You'll tell me soon."

I felt the rage gathering inside of me. I felt the deputy yank me to my feet again. I could feel the cross throbbing on my left hand. I turned to the deputy.

"Start walking," he said.

I watched myself knee him in the groin. The deputy doubled over, clutching his crotch. Then he reached for his weapon.

But I couldn't stop; I couldn't do anything except see red. It was like what happened in the sporting goods store, except ten times stronger. I kicked the weapon out of his hand and then concentrated all my energy on his being—and then I let him have it.

The force came out of me like a bolt from the hand of Zeus. The sheriff's deputy was blown backward off his feet, his arms windmilling until he landed against the side of the cliff. I felt the rage building up again when a blow hit me in the back of the head. I fell forward onto the dirt again.

I rolled over on my side and looked up. Sheriff Winters was over me. He put his boot on my neck and pressed down. I couldn't breathe, my hands were tied behind my back, and there was a row of sharp stones digging into my side. I winced, my face wrinkling into a grimace of pain, trying to summon whatever.

"Dammit," said the sheriff, "you can add that, kid. That was an assault on a police officer…"

Then he stopped talking. The pressure from the boot on my neck let up. I gasped as the air rushed back into my lungs.

I looked up at Sheriff Winters. A look of horror appeared on his face, and he was looking at something behind me. I felt the hairs on my neck and arms stand up. I attempted to roll over, but it was too hard with the handcuffs.

But I had a direct view of Cy and Arthur, and their faces were even more shocked than the sheriff's.

"What is it?" I whispered.

"It's Little Horn," said Cy.

CHAPTER SEVENTEEN

*L*ittle *Horn.*
  I jackknifed my body and rolled over into a crouch. With much difficulty, I tensed my abdominals and pulled myself up to my knees. Then I saw him, finally.

Roivas. Little Horn. Whatever you call him, he was unlike anything I'd seen before. We were the same age, but that's where the similarities ended. He wore a navy-blue pinstripe suit with shiny shoes. What made him so horrific were the rows of little horns sprouting out of his—its?—chest, back and shoulders. They'd punched straight through the suit, making him, or it, look like an evil, demented cactus. I looked into his face and felt sick to my stomach. It had distorted itself into a dark mass.

"Oh my good God," said Sheriff Winters, backpedaling.

Roivas took three steps toward the sheriff, who unholstered his weapon and tried to take aim with shaking hands, but Little Horn swept the weapon out of his hands.

"You'd better put away that Halloween costume and get down on your knees," said the sheriff, struggling to sound unfazed, tough.

Suddenly, Little Horn drew himself up to his full height. He went from six feet to nine feet in an instant. It was terrifying, and I got to my feet and ran back into the cave and threw myself onto the ground beside Arthur, who looked as terrified as I felt.

Sheriff Winters stood his ground and drew his baton. His hand was shaking.

I watched as Little Horn raised his arm, reared back, and swung hard at the sheriff. The row of small horns on his sleeve slashed across the sheriff's chest. Seven ribbons of red appeared and Sheriff Winters looked up with a dazed expression, then dropped to his knees and fell on his side.

Little Horn stepped forward and grabbed the man by the hair, then dragged him upright, the sheriff's legs trailing behind like a rag doll's in the dirt. Near the edge of the cliff, he let go, and the sheriff collapsed face-first on the ground. Then Little Horn went over to where the deputy had passed out and grabbed him by the hair and pulled him over to the sheriff. Their two bodies now lay side by side on the rock.

Little Horn turned and looked at Cy, Arthur and me. Its face was still a mass of dark anger; I couldn't make out anything human in the morphing features.

It pointed at us. Then it let loose a piercing sound so eerie that my bowels nearly emptied when I heard it. I found myself cowering with Arthur. Cy took several steps backward into the cave and stood in front of us.

Little Horn picked up the sheriff and deputy—one man in each hand—and leaped over the side of the cliff.

And he was gone.

Cy and I ran over to the edge and looked down. The side

of the mountain wasn't totally vertical here, but it was still very steep. There was a thick growth of trees on the valley floor, about two hundred yards below us.

"There," said Cy, pointing. "Little Horn dragged them there."

"Is he going to kill them?"

Cy looked at me. "He's been killing since the dawn of time. It's easy for him."

"Why didn't he kill us?"

"I don't know. It wasn't the time, I guess. Only he knows. But he will, soon, no doubt."

"How did he find us?" I said.

"It was you. You revealed yourself by using that power on the deputy. It drew him like a moth to the flame."

Down below us, I saw a tree shake. "We should get out of here."

"We might be able to get a lead on him, and maybe even lose him, as long as you don't expose yourself again."

"But how are we going to get out of these handcuffs?"

"I don't know. Sonny might be able to help. He's always full of surprises. We'll head over to his property."

"But we have to get the girls out first."

"Then hurry up."

I ran back inside the cave, past where Arthur sat miserable on a rock, to the tunnel entrance. I bent over and shouted. "Julia and Grace, we really have to go."

A moment later, Grace's tiny voice answered. "She's almost done with the sketches."

"Finish up," I shouted. "We have to go *now*. Hurry out."

"Okaaay," came Julia's voice. I wasn't looking forward to telling her what I'd just witnessed happen to her father.

I stood impatiently waiting at the mouth of the tunnel. It

seemed to be taking them forever.

"How's everything? You two coming?"

"This is really hard," said Julia's choked voice. "Can you come help us? I'm scared."

"I don't think so."

"This is really scary and I'm afraid to move."

I dropped my face to my chest and thought about it. I decided to enter and see how far I could make it with handcuffs on.

"Okay," I said, "I'm coming."

I crouched down and began moving in a frog squat. I knew the tunnel like the back of my own hands. It was hard going, and my neck was killing me. Then I got to the narrowest part—I was dreading this—and so I flopped forward on my face and chest. I began to worm with my hands behind me. The tunnel was so low here that my hands and handcuffs scraped on the ceiling. I felt the panic setting in, the claustrophobia, so I forced myself to move faster.

When I didn't think I could scoot anymore, the tight spot opened up, and dripping with sweat, I pulled myself to my feet and staggered, bent over, to the end of the tunnel.

Julia grabbed me as I emerged into the Hall of Knowledge. I noticed that they had already packed everything into the bag again.

"Who put you in handcuffs?" said Julia.

I closed my eyes, wishing I could be anywhere else at that moment, not to have to be the one. I found myself finally saying the right words. "Your father."

"What? He's here? Outside the cave?"

"Yeah," I said.

"Is he trying to arrest you?"

"He ... *was*."

I let the implications of that sink in. "He left?"

As Julia dove into the tunnel, an enormous thud shook the entire cave. A pair of small rocks dropped onto the floor from the ceiling.

"What was that?" said Grace.

"Little Horn is here," I whispered. "I used my power again and he found us."

Her face grew as white as a bone. "He knows you're here, and he knows I'm here."

Another thud echoed through the cavern. We both raised our faces to the ceiling, since it seemed to be coming from overhead.

Then it dawned on me. "He's trying to destroy the Hall of Knowledge."

Without another word, we both crouched over and ran into the tunnel.

The thudding grew stronger as we monkey-walked down the tunnel. I heard rock beginning to crash down onto the cave floor. "Here's the narrow part!" I shouted. "Down on your belly!"

Then I remembered the drawings.

Julia's work was packed inside a bag inside the trolley pan. Normally I would pull it through when finished, but with the chaos raining down inside the Hall of Knowledge, I wasn't sure there would be a Hall of Knowledge for much longer.

I turned and started back. "Where are you going?" she said.

"The drawings, I have to bring them by hand. You go. I'll catch up."

By the time I got back into Hall of Knowledge, an enormous crack was running down the center of the wall. The symbols had all vanished, almost the same way that a computer screen goes blank when it's been damaged.

The enormous thuds rattled my teeth as I arched my back and reached into the bag. At last I felt the drawings, and stood up again. Just as I turned back to the tunnel, a wide beam of sunlight exploded upon the wall over my head. A huge crack sounded behind me as a three-foot-wide stone landed on the ground and broke in two.

Overhead, a shaft of sunlight had appeared in the ceiling of the cave. Looking down was a silhouette with hundreds of small horns.

Roivas.

He was destroying the Hall of Knowledge to stop his enemies and to find me, or Grace, or both of us.

I bent over and raced into the tunnel. This would have to be the fastest passage of my life.

I sweated through the tight space, rippling my body. I was so panicked that I bashed my head on the rock. That stopped me for a moment. Lying inside the tunnel, I heard more pieces of the Hall of Knowledge crash to the ground behind me.

Then I heard something even worse—a piercing scream that came roaring down the tunnel from behind me. Roivas had seen the tunnel, and possibly glimpsed me.

Total panic. I got moving again, my insides a tangle of fury, and a few seconds later I had squeezed through the tightest part of the passage. I got to my feet and did the same awkward squat march down the remainder of the tunnel.

Behind me I could hear the gasps and the grunts and the shrieks of Roivas as he tried to fit himself through the tunnel. I didn't dare turn and look back. I stayed focused on reaching the small circle of gray light that was growing bigger with every shuffle.

Then another massive thud, and I heard a symphony of destruction explode behind me. A gust of wind blew out from the tunnel all around me, and my hair blew up around my face. A tube of brown dust billowed out, making me cough.

A moment later, I emerged from the tunnel, nearly puking, doubled over with the handcuffs behind me. I tried to stand up, but my legs were cramped, and I fell over instead. I held on to the drawings behind my back.

I felt hands on me, pulling me to my feet. It was Grace.

"He's trying to destroy the Hall of Knowledge."

"And he already did," I said, "but we saved the drawings."

I turned around, and she took the papers from my hand. "Where are the others?"

"They went down into the valley. Cy said that we can take shelter in the native cemetery."

We exited the cave and found the path to the right and moved quickly, hugging the edge of the cliff. The sounds of destruction grew farther behind us, and they were accompanied by an occasional whoop.

"It sounds like he's having fun destroying it," I said. "It's hard to believe that you were born brother and sister."

"Don't remind me. Anyway, it's only for this iteration."

A few minutes later, we came around a bend, and directly below us was the area of the valley that Sonny had pointed out to me. It was also the place where I'd bounced off the invisible barrier.

"I don't know what Cy has in mind, but this part of the valley is off limits to anyone who isn't a native," I said. "There's a strange force field around it."

"Maybe that's why Cy is doing that," she said. I followed her pointed finger to where Cy was on the ground, bowing his face, raising it to the sky, and repeating. Arthur and Julia sat nearby with their arms around one another.

We descended the scree-covered slope until we arrived at the group. Julia leaped to her feet and ran to deliver me a huge embrace. "We heard the destruction! You made it!"

"Barely," I said. "By about a minute. I had to go back to get your drawings." I nodded to Cy. "He's trying to drop the force field."

Julia nodded. "There's just so much to take in. Nothing is the way that I thought it was."

I nodded. "I felt the same way."

Cy paused his salutations, his face lifted to the sky. Then he nodded, and struggled to his feet. We were both handcuffed here, in the bottom of this beautiful valley. It was absurd.

"My ancestors have agreed to shelter us from Little Horn. Let's enter."

I gingerly stepped across the same patch of earth that had knocked me on my rear a few days earlier. There was no perimeter fence any longer. The five of us stepped onto the sacred land and looked around.

It seemed like any other plot of rural earth. Bushes and brambles lay strewn across the earth, patches of dirt were punctuated by clods of grass and weeds. I watched Julia bend down and pick up a pile of earth in her hands.

"I wouldn't do that," said Cy.

"Why not?"

"Those are my ancestors, and they're with us right now. We must show them respect."

She carefully set the dirt back down on the ground and stayed mum. She attempted to walk more lightly across the ground.

Meanwhile, I was growing more than tired of the handcuffs. In frustration, I tried turning around and scratching them off on a tree, but that just chewed up the bark.

Arthur looked at me sadly. "You can't get those off. I don't know what we're gonna do."

"We could find the sheriff and the deputy and get the key."

"I don't think they're alive," he said.

Julia was within earshot, so I nodded toward her. "Keep your voice down," I whispered.

"You can't go anywhere," said Cy, "not until we know that Little Horn has gone."

"How will we know that?"

"Sonny can feel his presence."

I spun around and looked up toward his ranch. "Can we get Sonny down here to tell us?"

"Oh, he'll see us," said the old native. "Remember, he's a seer. He sees everything in this valley. And he definitely heard the destruction of the Hall of Knowledge."

We stood there for a while, feeling the damp air, all casting glances over to the patch of forest that we'd seen Roivas disappear into with the sheriff and the deputy.

I saw that Julia had sat down on a fallen log and was hiding her face in her hands. I sat down next to her and pressed my shoulder against hers. "I'd like to put my arm around you, but, you know."

That got a smile out of her. She put her arm around me. "Is my dad okay, William?"

I felt my breath catch in my throat. "I don't think so."

I felt her tense up.

"William. What happened?"

"I'm sorry. There was nothing we could do."

"What *happened*?"

"Roivas. He slashed him."

She pulled her arm away and bent over in panic, saying, "Oh my God, please no," over and over again.

It was better that she knew. I didn't want her to be in suspense any longer, not about something like this.

"Roivas slashed him. Then he dragged your father and his deputy into those trees way over there."

She looked aghast. "What's wrong with you? We have to rescue him! That's my father!"

"What can I do?" I said. "Look at me. Look at Cy. And then look at Roivas. What can any of us do? That thing destroyed the entire Hall of Knowledge with its bare hands, from what I saw. I even saw it change shape." I shook my head. "That creature is too powerful for us to fight. Staying here for the moment is the best thing for all of us to do."

"But my father…"

"His fate is out of your hands."

She was crying now.

I knew what she was feeling, but I was powerless to help her or her father.

At that moment, another piercing shriek sounded from the forest. We all turned our heads.

Little Horn was marching out of the trees—and he was headed for us.

I shot to my feet, as did the others. Cy put out a calming hand toward all of us. "This cemetery is protected by my ancestors. He can't get through."

Arthur was trembling. "I wouldn't be so sure about that."

"It's true," I told him. "I tried to cross this land once, alone, and it was like walking into a piece of Plexiglas. I bounced right off it."

"But Roivas is more powerful than you," said Arthur.

"I guess that's the real question. Who's more powerful—Roivas or Cy's spiritual ancestors?"

We all fell quiet as Roivas crossed the landscape. It was like watching the Grim Reaper march toward you. If he could penetrate the force that protected the cemetery, it was certain we'd all be slaughtered. I didn't want to die, of course, but I had already faced so many threats and had my family murdered, and I felt that I should be more fearless, considering. But I wasn't. I was terrified to my core as I watched Roivas near the cemetery.

Roivas had returned to a normal human size, but the horns that had sprouted from his body were somehow sharper—and a few were smeared with blood.

I glanced over at Julia. The blood had drained out of her face—she was the picture of pure horror. Then I looked at Grace. This, after all, was her brother—or maybe *had been* would be the better way to say it. She was frightened, certainly, but she stared at Roivas with an expression more perplexed than scared.

I asked her, "Do you recognize him?"

Grace shook her head. "Not anymore. He looks totally different. I mean, those… horns." She grew quiet. "But I remember seeing them once, when we were little. We were wrestling at home, like brothers and sisters do, and I did something to him that he didn't like, and then I thought I saw a couple of them sprout on his back."

"Was he angry?"

She nodded. "That was just before he threw me against a wall. Our mother put him away on seventy-two-hour psychiatric hold."

"How old were you?"

"We were five."

That shocked me. A kindergartener on a psychiatric hold? The Other Side had come out early in him. I suddenly understood the type of mixed feelings Grace must've been carrying for all these years about her brother, Roivas. How difficult would it be knowing that your own brother was the embodiment of evil?

As Roivas drew nearer, the five of us instinctually huddled together. Then he suddenly stumbled backward. The wall.

"It held!" said Arthur.

"Wait," said Julia, "It's getting up again."

I watched as Roivas stood up and brushed off its navy-blue pinstripe suit. Its facial features were a strange blur of darkness and anger, as though its humanity had simply disappeared. I watched as it ran toward us again, and bounced off the wall even harder.

I looked over at Cy. He'd dropped to his knees and was moving his forehead to the earth, face to the sky, a back-and-forth routine. It seemed that he was supplicating his ancestors, pleading with them to stay strong.

Then Roivas stood up a third time. He faced the invisible wall, lifted his arms, and tilted his head back. A peculiar screech came from his throat that descended down to a guttural roar. I could feel the dark energy emanating from his body. Then he began walking, the roar still sounding from his throat—and then he crossed over the line.

"Oh crap," said Arthur.

"Cy, he's in!" I shouted. Cy looked up and a spasm of fear crossed his face.

We huddled together in a tight little group, facing Roivas as he crossed the expanse of brush. Raindrops spattered on my head and shoulders.

"What do we do?" shouted Julia.

Grace tugged on my sleeve. "Look."

She pointed ahead. An elderly figure had quietly crossed the graveyard and planted himself resolutely between our group and Roivas.

It was Sonny.

Cy shouted something in a language that I didn't understand. It must've been the native language of their people. With his back to us, Sonny merely lifted a hand, then lowered it again—an acknowledgment of the danger, it seemed, but a sign of disregard for his own safety.

I watched as Sonny pointed at Roivas. He began chanting something in that same language, first in a small voice, then in a louder one. Roivas grew taller again, returning to the nine-foot height, and Julia and Grace sucked in their breath. "I never saw him do that before," said Grace.

"He's more powerful than the last time you saw him."

"Much more powerful."

Sonny was still chanting. He held his thin body stock still, his spindly old-man arms trembling with the effort. Roivas twisted and writhed in front of him, then issued an ungodly shriek, lifted its right arm—and brought it down onto the top of Sonny's head.

The old man instantly crumpled to the ground. There wasn't any need to guess what had happened. That was a murder, plain and simple.

Sonny was dead. It was ghastly.

Julia gagged, then started to shudder and shake with intense panic. Grace put her arms around Julia and tried to calm her.

Roivas stepped on the body with a sickening *squish* and continued marching toward us. Cy's face was frozen with sheer terror. I'd never seen him like that. We bunched together in a tight knot.

"There must be something," said Arthur.

"Somebody stop him!" shouted Julia.

"Grace," I said, "you're his sister, at least you were in this iteration. Can you get to him somehow? Do you remember a cleaving point, a weakness?"

Next to me, Grace lowered her chin to her chest. Then she lifted her face. "Maybe there's one thing. I don't know if it will work. It sometimes worked when we were children."

"Try it!" said Arthur. "We're too young to die. Even Cy."

She took a deep breath, then broke from the huddle and

took a few steps forward. She was standing with her chest lifted and shoulders back. I knew that Roivas recognized her, because the ghastly figure stopped advancing. Its facial features seemed to reform on its face, and for the first time, I could see eyes, nose and mouth.

"Roland," she said.

"Grace," the creature replied—not in that deep "devil" voice I expected from the movies, but in thin, watery tones.

She stopped and said, "You leave these people alone. You don't need any of them."

He flexed his arms, and the horns withdrew and reappeared, much like a cat retracting its claws. "I do. I do, I do, I do, I do…"

When Grace opened her mouth next, her voice had utterly changed. It sounded like a grown man's voice. "You go to the Purespace."

"No, I won't…"

"Yes, you will. The Purespace. *Now.*" Her voice dropped so low on that last word that it gave me shivers.

Roivas moved forward, and she repeated, "Purespace," forcefully. "That's where Proof is."

He attempted to move toward her, but he faltered, leaped into the air and shrieked, loud enough to echo off the sides of the valley. It flexed its horns. Its face was disappearing and reappearing, as though it were involved in some horrific identity crisis.

"I don't want the purespace or Proof!" it cried. "That's *your* space! I don't want it!"

"Then *go*," said Grace, pointing her finger out of the valley.

Roivas was in the middle of what appeared to be a massive temper tantrum. The creature whirled, stamped its feet, and blasted apart bushes with fireballs. It brought its fists down onto a nearby boulder, splitting it in half. It roared again and again. Finally, it scooped what seemed to be half a ton of earth and threw it at us.

I stood there, cowering with the group. We protected our heads while the cloud of dirt rained down upon me. After it had cleared, we opened our eyes.

Roivas was gone.

Before us, Grace slowly turned around. She looked like she was about to faint. Then she did. I watched her knees buckle and her eyes shut and then her whole body go sideways. I rushed over, but Arthur and Julia, with their arms free, were the only ones who could attend to her.

"Oh my gosh, how did she *do* that?" asked Julia.

Arthur propped Grace's head in his hands. The girl soon opened her eyes and blinked twice, then looked around at our faces.

"Grace, you are a wizard," said Arthur. "But what is a purespace?"

A faint smile spread across her face. "I could see that there was a little bit of Roland left inside of him, but not much. So I threatened him with the punishment that our father used to use."

"You sounded like a man," said Arthur.

"I can change my voice. It's part of my power." She exhaled. "I'm surprised it worked. But it won't work again. I could feel that there's almost nothing left of Roland. In a little while, he'll be all Roivas."

"Little Horn," said Cy pensively. He looked at the mutilated body of Sonny nearby. "That was my friend. He didn't deserve to die like that. We must bury him."

We stood there, breathing in the rain, trying not to look at the man's undignified remains.

Arthur was the first one to break the silence. "So what do we do now?"

"I know," I answered. "We try to find Julia's dad to get the key for these handcuffs."

"If he's alive," Arthur whispered to me.

"Even if he isn't," I whispered back.

"Julia, you stay here," I said. "Cy and Grace, you stay too. Arthur and I will go up to the forest."

They all nodded. Arthur and I began to make our way across the field, picking through the stones and the brambles. We must've been quite a sight—me in my handcuffs, him with the bandage around his torso.

"I bet you didn't see this coming when you hopped into the truck yesterday," I said.

"Dude, there's no way I'm going back to school. This has, like, blown my mind. Roivas was *sick*."

"I could see his face forming when Grace stood in front of him," I said.

"I know, me too. Do you think he's like an ancient power?"

I didn't answer that. The answer would've been really long, and I didn't know enough about Roivas and Change Agents and the history of evil in the universe to do it justice anyway.

We picked our way up to the edge of the forest. "If they're alive, they're probably freaked out—and they have weapons."

Arthur understood. We stepped lightly through the copse of trees, our footsteps muffled on the pine needles. Our heads swiveled from left to right and back again, looking for anything that might resemble a law-enforcement officer.

Then I spotted it. The khaki uniform, lying on the floor of the forest. I knew he was dead even before we reached him. It was clear from the unnatural way that he was twisted on the ground.

As we drew closer, I saw that it was the deputy. His throat had been slashed, and he'd bled out right there on the forest floor. The animals would be arriving soon, I knew.

"Can you find the keys?" I said.

"I don't know where they are."

"They're on his belt."

"But where on his belt?"

"I don't know. Just unlatch the belt and we'll take the whole thing. We might need the weapons too."

Arthur reached under the deputy's body and unlatched the police belt and pulled it out. Then he laid it out on the ground, and we looked down at the hardware. I spotted the keys and nudged them with the toe of my shoe. "There they are."

My friend grunted and pulled them out of the belt. I turned around, and Arthur fumbled at my wrists for a few seconds. Then I heard a click and felt the handcuffs fall away. It felt incredibly freeing. I walked around, flexing my arms, trying to get the blood moving again.

Arthur slung the dead deputy's belt around his own waist. Then he looked at me. "So where's the sheriff?"

"I don't know," I said. "He's got to be here somewhere."

"If he's dead too, he's got to be nearby. He got slashed across the chest."

We began to search for the sheriff, fanning out in every direction, but neither of us had any luck.

"Maybe he survived and ran away," I said.

"That's doubtful. I wonder if Roivas ate him."

"Bones and all?"

We looked at each other. Nobody had told me any stories about Little Horn and cannibalism, but that didn't mean it *couldn't* happen.

"Let's head back and unlock Cy," I finally said.

We turned and went back down the same way we had come. When we arrived at the graveyard, we stepped through the invisible wall. The others were waiting for us, and as Arthur unlocked Cy's handcuffs, Julia grabbed my arm. "Did you find him?"

"We found the deputy, but not your dad. We have no idea what happened to him."

I looked into those hopeful eyes and added, "Maybe he got away!"

Her eyes lit up at that—a tiny beacon of hope. I was glad to give it to her.

We stood there, free of handcuffs, the five of us alive and, except for Arthur's apparently broken rib, more or less no worse for wear.

"You guys," said Arthur, "what happened to Sonny?"

He was pointing to where the old neighbor had fallen. A few minutes ago, we'd seen his mutilated body. Now it was gone—vanished from inside his clothing. All that was left was his shirt and pants, lying flat on the dirt.

"You buried him already?" I said. It didn't seem possible.

"No, we didn't touch him," said Grace. "He must've just vanished."

Cy looked very satisfied and not in the least bit surprised. "We're in the graveyard of our ancestors. They take care of us."

I ran a hand through my hair and gazed around. This was truly hallowed ground, and I reconsidered my skepticism about all those old stories that native people have about skin walkers and other such creatures. If Roivas could exist and if Sonny's body could disappear, then anything could happen.

"You've seen this happen before?" I asked.

"Well, no," he admitted, "this is the first time. But we've always held on to the stories."

"Cy, William and I were able just to walk back into the graveyard," said Arthur. "Does that mean that it's open now?"

Cy looked sad and closed his eyes. I sensed that he was communing with something unseen. Then he opened his eyes. "My ancestors tell me that Roivas has polluted this place. It isn't protected anymore."

"So we can't escape Roivas here," I said.

"We never really did," said Julia. "He broke right through it."

"And my little trick won't work again," said Grace.

"So what can we do to defeat this guy?" I asked. "What in the world do we possess that can defeat Roivas?"

"Little Horn cannot be defeated in this realm," said Cy. "That's what we've always been told."

"Then where can we defeat him?" Arthur asked.

That's when the answer hit me. I stared at Arthur, trying to get him to understand. "Why are you looking at me, dude?"

"Think about it, Arthur."

"Think about what?"

I grew impatient. "What did I ask you to help me with last week?"

My friend looked confused. "The helmets."

"Exactly."

Recognition dawned in his eyes. "It's the helmets."

I turned and spoke to the others. "You remember how I asked Arthur to help me build helmets? And how they appeared to me in a dream?"

"It was the L.E. who showed you," said Grace.

"Who's the L.E.?" asked Julia.

It would take too long to explain. "I'll tell you later. But I think they were trying to tell me something."

"The L.E. were trying to tell you how to defeat Little Horn," said Arthur.

"Exactly."

We stood, still unsure of where to go, or what to do. "So you built them?" asked Cy.

"Yes, but they don't work. We're missing something, and I don't know what to do."

Arthur scratched his head with his good arm, then pinched his nose. "I mean we don't have much choice. The helmets seem like the best way to go forward."

"It does," said Grace.

I turned around and left the group. The drizzle started again, and I kicked a small stone with the toe of my shoe, and it skittered forward and landed inside a ring of bigger stones. They weren't covered by dirt and looked like they'd been placed there recently.

Then something came back to me. Inside the Hall of Knowledge had been a row of three images—a human skull, a circle of stones, and a small rectangle.

I was in a graveyard. That was a circle of stones. All that was missing was something rectangular.

That was the sign I needed, and I understood. The skull represented the native graveyard. The circle was the circle of stones. And the rectangle was something that I would find in the center.

I dropped to my knees, knowing full well how stupid I was going to look, and began pulling the dirt out from the center of stones. The others saw what I was doing and rushed over.

"William, that's sacred earth," said Cy.

"I'm treating it respectfully."

"Have you lost your mind?" asked Arthur.

"Trust me. I think this could be something."

To my surprise, Julia dropped to her knees beside me and

started digging too. Then Grace did the same.

"What are we looking for?" Julia asked.

"Something rectangular, but I don't know exactly what," I said. I explained the symbols that I'd seen on the wall of the Hall of Knowledge.

"I remember those," she said. "The skull, the circle, the rectangle."

"Hey, I found something," said Grace. Her fingers were running along the edge of something linear. "It feels like maybe a box."

The three of us gently removed the dirt from atop the object, and indeed it turned out to be a small box, maybe four inches by three inches wide. Our fingers worked quickly to excavate the dirt around the side of the item, and soon we'd lifted it out of the ground. I grew excited to look at it.

I turned to Cy, who was watching the whole pursuit with skepticism written across his craggy face. "Could this be a grave, Cy? Maybe the ashes of somebody?"

The old native thought carefully before he replied. "No, I don't think so. Burning the corpses isn't part of our tradition."

"Something's embossed on the top of the lid," said Grace. She wiped off the last remaining bits of dirt, and I saw something that startled me.

It was a cross. The same cross that had appeared on my left hand. I looked down at the mark on my hand, and it was pulsing.

Grace's eyes grew wide as she grabbed my hand and held it next to the lid. "Oh my gosh, William—you were right."

"Who's going to open it?" said Arthur.

"I'm kind of scared," said Julia. "A demon could fly out."

"We've already seen one of those today," I said. "But remember that the Hall of Knowledge gave me this clue. And they're on our side."

"Who is they?" said Julia.

"The L.E.," said Grace. "They were the first civilization to reach Final Ignition. They're trying to help us."

I reached for the box and opened the lid and looked down. My eyes widened, and I reached down and produced a small rectangular piece of blue plastic, no bigger than a thumbnail. I knew immediately what it was, and so did Arthur.

Our eyes met.

"It's a flash drive!" he said.

CHAPTER EIGHTEEN

I examined the thing. It looked like a normal thumb drive, except it didn't have any brand markings. And the casing didn't feel like plastic—it felt more durable, appeared to be more light absorbent, something the likes of which I'd never seen, probably from some place I'd never heard of.

"This is a gift to humanity," I said.

"Maybe someone just dropped it," said Arthur.

I looked up at him. "Are you a complete idiot?"

"I'm just saying that…"

"Someone dropped it?"

With a shrug, he said, "Yeah, I guess not."

"Anyway, nobody gets into this graveyard. Right, Cy?"

"That's right," the old man agreed. "That was placed there by something more powerful than even my ancestors."

"We need a computer to access it. I don't have one here. Julia?"

She shook her head. "I left mine at home yesterday."

"Grace?"

"Now who is the idiot?"

"Yeah—coma, hospital—sorry. Arthur?"

He pinched his lips tightly together and didn't speak.

"Did you bring your computer?" I said.

Pointing at the flash drive, he said, "I'm not putting that thing in my computer! It could, like, detonate or something."

"Arthur! Are you freaking kidding me? You're gonna save your computer and get us and maybe the whole world killed? You have some kind of hidden head injury?"

Staring at his shoes, Arthur mumbled, "Just that, I paid a lot for that computer. Have all my stuff in there…"

He looked up at us, all staring at him like he had lost his mind. "All right, all right! I'll try it, and we'll see what happens."

An hour later, we'd marched back up from the valley to Cy's cabin. We gathered around the fireplace while Cy put some logs into it but kept an eye outside for any nasty visitors. Grace put some hot water in a teapot, and Julia hid herself under a heavy blanket. We were all too stunned to talk much.

Arthur reached into his backpack and pulled out his laptop. He sat down on a tree stump that Cy liked to use for a stool, and put the computer on a side table. He opened the lid and pushed the power button.

I took a seat on a folding chair at his side. He looked at me, still stupidly worried about his computer. But I didn't want to lose Arthur's friendship, no matter how much this experience changed us.

He opened up his laptop, and when the background came up, he put his hand out. I gingerly put the flash drive in his palm. He loaded it into the side of his computer and crossed his fingers.

"This could be the end of all my work," he said.

"Or the salvation of civilization," I said.

The notice came up that a device had been found in the :E drive. Arthur clicked "open file."

We both leaned forward. A folder appeared on the screen. I held my breath, waiting for the file name to appear.

There was only one file in the folder. It was labeled with a single word.

Helmets.

"I can't believe it," I nearly shouted. I stood up and punched my fist into the air. "It wasn't a random dream. Someone was trying to contact me."

The others crowded around the screen. Cy stroked his chin and murmured something I couldn't understand. Julia and Grace were rapt. "Open it!" said Julia.

"I'm scared," said Arthur. "Like, what if that Roivas put it there? What if it's a trick, huh, and this opens a virus that somehow blows up the earth? Who's the idiot then?"

The rest of us exchanged glances. Hadn't considered that scenario.

Finally, I said, "Do it. It's all we got."

Arthur looked around at the others and double-clicked on the icon. A message on the screen said the program used to open the file wasn't detected, and asked which program should be used.

"Just click on any one," I said, impatiently.

"This is important," said Arthur.

"We have no idea what's inside, so it doesn't matter."

"Fine," he said, annoyed, "let's use Notepad."

"Nobody uses Notepad," said Julia.

"Developers do. It's as close to empty as you can get."

The file popped up, and it turned out to be nothing more than a long string of numbers. It didn't make any sense to my eyes, but I could see Arthur scanning the numbers.

"It a code," he said.

"Do you think you can crack it?"

"I don't know. I've never tried. I mean, I've done some basic programming, but this could be using a language we've never seen before."

We continued standing around him. I was practically breathing down his neck.

He turned around, and his eyes scanned ours. "Can you give me a little bit of room here?"

"Sorry," I said.

We all backed away. Later that night, the last thing I saw as I fell asleep on the mattress was Arthur hunched over, laboring on the code.

I woke up at seven o'clock the next morning to the feeling of a hand on my shoulder. I opened my eyes and saw Arthur's goofy face staring down at me. He looked maniacal but exhilarated.

"I did it," he said.

He was whispering so as not to disturb the others. I rubbed the sleep out of my face.

"Where is your computer?"

"Outside. I was working on the porch."

I hauled myself to my feet. Outside, I saw a heavy blanket on the porch rocking chair and the laptop on the tree stump. "You've been sitting out here all night?"

"Yeah, I kind of like the way that it feels out here. It's like working in nature. Though a few times I thought the crazy bastard was coming to kill us. Turned out to be rabbits. Let me show you what I got."

We looked at his screen together. "The files on this little

flash drive are blowing my mind."

"Why?" I asked.

"They're written in a programming language that I've never seen before. It's like an alien script."

I muttered agreement with that. Everything I'd experienced had felt nearly supernatural, yet scientific at the same time. At a certain point, the two lines converge. I remembered reading a famous science fiction writer who said that any sufficiently advanced technology is indistinguishable from magic.

"So anyway, I used portions of this code and compared it to some of the programming that I had in a file on my hard drive." He paused and looked at me. "William, how technical do you want me to get?"

"I don't understand any of it," I said truthfully. "Could you just summarize?"

He nodded. "The code is assembled from letters in every language in the world."

"That's incredible."

"It's like, what's the name of that global language that somebody invented in the nineteenth century? The one nobody uses?"

I thought about it. "Esperanto?"

"It's like Esperanto, except for programming."

"But what does it *say*, Arthur? About the helmets?"

He drew a deep breath. "I'm not done entirely with translating everything, but I *think* these are instructions for construction."

"Of the helmets?"

"Yes."

I whistled low through my teeth and stared at the long string of characters on the page. They looked like gobbledygook to me, but to problem solvers like Arthur they represented a delicious challenge.

"When do you think it'll be finished?"

"Maybe a few more hours. It depends on whether or not I get

breakfast."

I could take a hint and got to my feet again. "I'll handle that. You keep working."

He grinned, and we high-fived. Then Arthur winced and clutched the side of his chest. "Ow, that really hurts."

"It could've been a lot worse," I said.

"I'd love a Tylenol."

"I'd love to get you one," I said, "but it's too dangerous for us to leave this reservation right now. We've got a dead deputy and a missing sheriff."

I went to the kitchen and found the box of our food supplies on Cy's counter. I pulled out the pancake mix and poured it into a chipped mixing bowl and then looked for milk and eggs in Cy's refrigerator. I found them, and soon I was dripping the batter into a hot oiled pan. In the back of the refrigerator, I found some bacon that looked all right, and I had that sizzling too.

I could see Julia starting to stir nearby. Bacon was nature's alarm clock. "Breakfast," I said.

"I don't know if I can eat," she said sadly, and I knew she was thinking of her father, and I thought of mine.

Finally, I said, "Where's Grace?

"Right here." Julia rolled over. The other side of the mattress was empty.

"Um, I *thought* she was right here."

I stared at her. "Did she get up and leave in the middle of the night?"

"Don't know."

That was alarming. "Breakfast!" I hollered to Arthur. I knew that would get him inside, and it did. As I laid the first stack of hotcakes on a plate, he came rumbling in. I had something else on my mind.

"Arthur, have you seen Grace?"

"Yeah," he said, wolfing the pancakes into his mouth.

"When?"

"She went outside in the middle of the night."

I heard alarm bells starting to sound in my head.

"Did she tell you anything about where she was going?"

He looked up, chewing, and thought about it. "She said something, but I wasn't really listening."

Arthur was very smart, in his own way, but often clueless, and no more so than now.

"You let her go? Are you frickin' crazy?"

He looked up at me, guilty faced. "I thought she had to pee!"

"But when she didn't come back? What did you think then?"

"I—I'm sorry! I got caught up in the computer!"

I nodded and sighed, put a hand on his shoulder. "I know. Eat."

We all sat around the small dining table, eating. Well, I wasn't. My thoughts were preoccupied with Grace.

Cy entered. He had a dirty canvas bag over his shoulder that he threw onto the floor with a thump.

"Good morning," he said.

"Cy, we can't find Grace."

His face fell. "She went out somewhere?"

"Maybe. She left in the middle of the night, and nobody knows where she is."

"Oh boy," he said.

"Have some pancakes," I said.

He headed over to the kitchen, washed his hands, put some pancakes on his plate, and came and sat down with us. All four of us sat in silence, nothing but the sounds of silverware scraping against plates.

Then Cy slowed down. His eyes had fixed on something distant.

"What is that?" he said.

I followed his gaze. His finger went up and pointed toward a piece of paper on the mantle above the fire. It had been propped vertically, in a conspicuous way, so that we would see it.

"That's not mine," he said.

"Or mine," I said.

Arthur echoed it, and Julia shook her head no. I stood up and went over to the paper. My name was written on the front. *William.*

I turned it over. Three sentences.

I'm sorry but now that Roivas knows that I'm here he's going to be back and I don't want to put any of you in danger. I'm returning to the spiritual realm until we can sort all this out. Don't look for me. —Grace

I stood there looking at the paper. Grace was gone. Seemed like I had just found her, and she was gone. Gone to save our butts. My heart sank. She and I were one, somehow. I didn't know if that meant as friends or something more, but we were interconnected, emotionally inseparable. I focused, trying to tune her in. But it was clear that she was shutting me out.

"What does it say?" Julia asked.

"She's gone," I said.

"Where?"

I crossed the floor back to the table and handed the note to her. Julia read it, and a look of surprise passed over her face. "What's the spiritual realm?"

Cy and Arthur took turns reading it, and soon a pall had descended upon the room. "It's where we found her," said Cy.

"She was communicating with William from the other side."

Julia still didn't understand. "But what about her body? Is she dead?"

"She was in a coma," I explained. "She was communicating with me telepathically."

Arthur's eyes had grown wide. "So she's lying around somewhere nearby in a coma again."

"Probably," I muttered.

"A self-induced coma," he said.

I nodded. Cy sucked on his teeth. "What's the status of that flash drive, William?" I described everything that Arthur and I had been discussing. "So you're trying to translate the document?"

Arthur nodded. "It's going pretty slow, but I think it'll be done by this afternoon."

Cy held his palms open to the three of us. "I know that you probably want to find Grace, right?"

"Yeah," said Julia. "We can't just let her freeze. She could be dying out there—like my dad."

Cy shook his head. "She's a C.A. 3. If she went into the spiritual realm, there was a legitimate reason for it. Like she said, she's the attractor for Roivas, because they share so much, even, I guess, DNA."

"So what do you recommend?" asked Arthur.

Cy paused, then said, "I'd recommend that we leave her be, for now, wherever she is. Like she said. Instead, let's focus on building those helmets, and if they work, then whoever puts on the helmet can communicate with her in the spiritual realm."

Arthur was nodding his head. I admitted that it made sense. Only Julia looked unconvinced. "What can I do? I don't know anything about helmets."

"You could look for your dad," I said.

"My dad is fine," she said resolutely.

"Then we'll find things for you to do," said Cy.

At that, Arthur set down his silverware, wiped his mouth, and clapped his hands together. "I've got to get back to the code-cracking."

We stood up, but when I looked back, Julia was still in her seat, looking pensive.

Six hours later, I was chopping wood out in the back clearing when Arthur came shambling through the trees toward me.

I'd learned how to cut wood earlier, during my month-long stay with Cy, since he used only wood to heat the cabin. He'd showed me how to use an old tree stump as a stage of sorts. I learned how to put the chunks of wood on the stump and use the splitter to find any weakness in the wood. Then I learned the right way to lift the sledge over my head, how to drop it down powerfully, and where to connect it with the splitter. After some practice, I was able to cleave the pieces cleanly in half. The first time I tried it, I wasn't even able to lift the hammer. Now, I felt like an expert.

I did my last drop and watched the chunks fall to the left and the right. I leaned the sledgehammer against the tree stump.

Arthur arrived. I noticed the laptop was under his arm. "What's going on?"

"I did it," he said.

"You translated the whole document to English?"

He nodded. "I had to write my own program. That actually is what took all the time. Once I hit run, it translated the document in five seconds."

"Show me, you frickin' genius, you."

"Can you clean off that stump?"

I used my sleeve to clean all the wood shavings off the surface. They had a clean, piney smell. Arthur then set down the laptop, and we both sat down cross-legged on the ground.

He opened the case, entered his password, and then pulled up a document. It was only three hundred words.

"Read it and tell me what you think," he said.

My eyes scanned the document. The text contained odd phrases, as though an alien had, in fact, written it.

Arthur seemed to read my mind. "It sounds a little odd, but that's because of my program."

"It does sound weird," I said. "This part especially, where it says push the bubble in and it pops out and you are there."

He stroked his chin. "I don't think bubble is the best translation for whatever they were trying to say. But it sounds like that's the last step."

He and I went over the previous stuff together. To my surprise, I found that Arthur had been remarkably close on his first attempt with the helmets. His instincts to use all the latest in paranormal-research technology, particularly electrostatics, was dead on, it seemed.

After more discussion, I thought I had a good handle on things. "So let me see if I can understand this," I said. "You need to fix two major things. One is the compression."

"Which I knew, but this document tells me exactly how."

I nodded. "Two, you have to fiddle with the frequencies."

"I had them set at 540 hertz. When that didn't work, I had them set at 560 hertz. What I didn't realize was that there needs to be one of each, because the difference between them will make a third tone of 20 hertz that will transport the user to the spirit realm."

That sounded plausible to me. "If that's what the instructions say, then we do it. So what now?"

"We need to make these changes. You brought the tools, right?"

A sinking feeling settled into the pit of my stomach. I lowered my face to the ground and ran a hand through my hair.

"No, I forgot."

A wave of frustration crossed Arthur's face. I noticed that he seemed to have lost weight, even just in the last few days. "I reminded you to bring them, William."

"I know, I know." I stood up and walked over to the other side of the glen. Moodily, I picked up a pine cone and chucked it as far as I could into the trees. "I made a mistake. I'm not perfect."

He sighed. "Well, is there some place else we could find tools?"

I thought about it; then the answer came to me. "Yes, there is."

"Where?"

"Sonny had a workshop on his property."

An hour later, we had scrambled down the side of the valley and up to the other side. As usual, the soil got under my fingernails, and the knees of my pants were caked in dirt.

This particular hike was even more difficult because I was dragging behind me a large canvas bag holding the two helmets. Arthur was carrying his backpack around the front of his body, as though it contained a royal crown. Which it kind of did. To my eyes, the document detailing how to make these helmets was more valuable than anything else on earth.

We arrived at Sonny's property. It looked the same as the

first time that I'd visited there. The rocking chair sat on the porch, untouched. Somewhere in the distance behind the house a dog was barking.

To the left stood the little shack containing his workshop. I noticed a lock on the door latch.

"This is it," I said to Arthur.

"Do we just break in?"

"I guess we have to."

Arthur unslung the backpack from his torso and set it gingerly on the ground. Then he turned to the door and charged toward it with his shoulder, like they do in the movies.

He collided with the door and bounced off it. His mouth opened, and he rubbed his right shoulder with his left hand. "Oh crap—that hurt!"

"You're supposed to use your foot," I said, "like this."

I set down the bag containing the helmets. Then I positioned myself in front of the door, took a deep breath, and did my best karate kick at the latch. I felt the pain shoot through my ankle and up my leg, and I fell backward on the dirt. The door didn't budge.

"We're amazing," said Arthur. "Just unbelievable idiots."

I got up from the dirt and limped around on my gimpy ankle for a minute. "You have any better ideas?"

He looked around. I saw his gaze fall upon something on the porch. "Yeah, I do."

He walked over to Sonny's porch and bent down and hoisted up a large rock, about the size of a fire hydrant. I was surprised that Arthur could even hoist that much weight, but sometimes a person can surprise you with hidden strength.

He hobbled back over, his feet splayed wide, so that he was walking like a penguin, the rock held in front of his pelvis. He proceeded directly to the workshop door, stopped a couple feet in front of it, and began to swing the rock back and forth between his legs.

"Arthur, I don't know if that's—"

I never finished my sentence, because on the third swing, he suddenly threw the rock toward the door. It crashed through the wooden slats as if they were made of straw and left a gaping hole in the middle of the door.

"Ladies first," he said, gesturing to the hole.

I high-fived Arthur, kicked in a few more wooden slats with the heel of my shoe, then ducked my head and stepped inside Sonny's workshop.

It was a dark little place. I couldn't see a thing at first, but I could feel that it had been used a lot over the years. The bitter taste of metal seeped into my mouth, and the scent of iron filings filled my nose. A stray cobweb brushed across my cheek, causing me to splutter and pass my hands across my face.

After a minute, my eyes adjusted to the darkness. There was a workbench, a sawhorse, and a long table over which hung a long rack filled with at least a hundred different tools. There were bent-nose pliers, long-nose pliers, Allen wrenches, seven types of hand crimpers, insulation strippers, bolt cutters, and innumerable pliers. I spotted a chainsaw, a spot-welding mask, and a table-mounted vise.

"This place has everything," said Arthur. "Utility knives, levels, squares…"

I pulled the overhead light string. The bulb didn't turn on. "Everything except electricity."

Arthur was already busy rustling through the bins on the ground. "That's okay, there's a generator here. I bet that Sonny never had electricity here except for that."

I looked over his shoulder at the generator. It was an ancient contraption, a rusted yellow box surrounded by protective black bars. Some kind of acid had corroded the surface so that it looked like insects had eaten it.

"What does it run on?" I said.

"Gas. I hope there's enough inside. Man, I can't see anything in here."

He fumbled around, threw a few buttons, flipped the red power switch, and yanked a cord. The generator sputtered to life. Arthur then connected the long extension cord from the light to the generator. The bulb lit up.

"You won't have any problem seeing now," I said.

He clapped his hands together. "Where are my patients? The surgeon is in."

I went outside and brought in the bag with the helmets and laid them on Sonny's worktable. Arthur was already assembling tools. "Whoa! A hydraulic torque wrench."

"Those aren't unusual."

"I know. But they're just cool."

He brought over a tray full of hex nuts, acorn nuts, flat washers, hex heads, and Allen heads. Then he rolled up his sleeves.

"The operation is ready to begin. Surgeon requests that everybody leave the operating theater except for essential staff."

I nodded and backed out of the workspace. It was better to leave Arthur to his expertise. If he needed me, I was just a shout away.

Sonny's house was locked up. I decided not to try to get inside, having done enough damage to the dead man's workshop.

So I wandered his property for a while, looking at the belongings of this elderly Native American. There was a bench under an oak where I anchored down for a while. A weathered garden gnome in a patch of wild mint occupied my thoughts for another while. I even stooped over to pull a few weeds out of a garden bed. I don't know why I did that. In a few weeks, the weeds would overgrow the property.

The nagging question was what had happened to Sonny's body. I knew that Cy had taken his clothing and buried it in the place where he'd been killed. That was no mystery at all. But the way he'd just vaporized or combusted or decayed was one of the strangest things I'd ever seen, and nothing could explain it.

Then I went and stood on the small ridge and looked out over the valley. It was the same ridge that I had stood on with Sonny, and the same place where Sonny had pointed out the cemetery to me.

At that moment, I noticed something odd. On the other side of the valley, nearer to Cy's cabin, a commotion was occurring. I could see movement, several figures running through the forest.

A glint of chrome caught my eye. A flash of metal. Khaki uniforms, tall hats. I understood what that was.

The sheriff's deputies had arrived.

Sheriff Winters could be alive, or he could be dead. Either way, he'd likely told his deputies exactly where he was going, and why. If he hadn't come back, they probably decided to find out why—and were looking specifically for me and Arthur and Julia. If he had survived Little Horn—Roivas—somehow, and he had gone back, then they'd be looking for Little Roivas. In which case, I wished them luck.

But either way, I wasn't going to cross that valley and find out. I hurried back to the workshop and stepped inside. "Arthur,"

I said, "we've got some company."

He looked up from the bench. The guts of the helmets were spilling out onto the table. "Who?"

"The sheriff's deputies," I said. "They're swarming Cy's property across the way."

His eyes flashed. "What do you want me to do about that?"

"Work faster," I said.

"I'm trying," he said, "but it's not exactly easy to work here." As if on cue, the light bulb flickered out, and he kicked the generator with his foot. It started up again.

"All I need is for those helmets to be functional," I reminded him. "If you can make that happen, I enter the spiritual realm, find Grace, and defeat Little Horn or Roivas or whatever thousand other things people call the nasty little bastard."

"You make it sound so easy," he said.

He was right. I admitted to myself that it wasn't going to be that easy. But if Cy was right, and if the Hall of Knowledge was right, it was the most important thing in the world to do.

Because it would mean the salvation of our civilization.

I waited impatiently near the ridge. I couldn't stand directly on it for fear that the deputies would see me. There was no sign of Cy or Julia, and I wondered if they'd heard the deputies coming and scattered. If so, they were possibly hiding in the forest.

There was nothing for me to do but wait for Arthur to finish. I was fidgety, agitated. The police presence on this reservation seemed unnecessary, a distraction from my real purpose here. I felt like they didn't know what they were getting involved in.

To some extent, neither did I.

After another hour, I spotted the deputies starting to spread down the far valley slope. They were going slowly, picking their way. I could tell that they were doing a search.

I ran back to the workshop and stepped inside. Arthur was spot-welding something on the antennae, the heavy mask over his face, the tool making a *bzzzt* sound.

"Arthur, can I help?"

He shut off the tool and flipped up his mask. The light bulb went out, and the room was plunged into darkness. He kicked the generator, and it turned on again. "No need, William. I just finished."

"The helmets are done?"

He lifted one. "The helmets are done."

I approached him and picked one up. I could see that he'd certainly made some changes to the configuration; he'd stripped out some of the wiring and also added a clear Plexiglas shield to the front visor.

"What's this?"

"That's something that was in the document. It said that there needed to be something to protect the person. In case you spend a long time on the other side."

I hoisted the thing and put it on my head. It fit snugly. My fingers felt along the side of the helmet for the power button.

"Can I?"

He bowed theatrically. "It would be an honor. This was your idea, after all."

I hit the power button on the side of the helmet—and the world disappeared.

I find myself in a world of absence. All around me is the thickened, soupy grayness of an indistinguishable place. I can't smell or hear anything. I raise my hand and look down. There is no hand.

Then I open my mouth to speak but can't feel that either. No sound comes out. My eyes focus on the two blinking blue lights above my eyes. That's my helmet. There's almost nothing else.

A woman's face appears before me.

William, Grace says.

I start to say her name—and then everything disappears.

I found myself on the floor of the workshop. My left arm pinned under my body and my legs turned awkwardly inward. I flicked my eyes to the right. Arthur was crouched over me, holding the helmet under his arm.

"What happened?" I said.

"Dude, you dropped to the ground like a sack of dog crap."

"Dog crap?"

He shrugged. "Just came to mind."

"When did I drop?"

"Like, the second you hit the power button. Did it work?"

I struggled to roll over, but my body felt mildly paralyzed. It felt as though someone had injected cold gel into all of my joints. "Yeah it worked," I said. "I was standing in a—I don't know—a gray zone. I couldn't see or feel my own body." I looked down at my body. "Kind of like now. Can you help me up?"

Arthur put his arm underneath my body and helped me up. I held on to the side of the table for balance until I felt everything coming back to life.

"How long was I gone?"

"Ten seconds. When you fell, I ran around the table and shut the helmet off."

It was stunning to hear I'd lost most of my body processes in such a short amount of time. I understood now why Grace had been in such a comatose state when I'd found her.

"So that's why the L.E. showed me a helmet," I said. "For protection."

"No doubt."

"Let's go outside."

We stepped outside of the workshop, into Sonny's front yard area. The sky was darkening again, and I felt a spatter of rain upon my face. I stood there with my hands on my waist, looking around.

"The last thing I saw was Grace's face," I said. "She appeared to me just before you cut the power."

"That's radical," he said. "Where do you think her body is?" Arthur looked around. "Maybe she's just lying on the forest floor someplace."

"She's smarter than that," I said. "She probably put herself somewhere where she is safe. We'll have to do the same."

A female voice called. "There you two are!"

Arthur and I spun around. Julia had appeared on the crest of the ridge. She was out of breath and looking bedraggled. There were bits of grass and twigs stuck to her clothing.

"Julia!" I said.

I ran toward her and threw my arms around her. "We saw the deputies. I was worried about you."

"Oh my gosh," she said, "I wanted to talk to them to find out about my dad, but Cy told me I couldn't go."

That did seem like a conflict of interest. I could imagine that Julia didn't take too kindly to being told that she couldn't ask the deputies about her father.

"So what did you do?"

"I was freaking out, so Cy made me calm down. Then he took us down into a hiding place. It's somewhere over there." She gestured to the high forest above the crumbled Hall of Knowledge, an area I hadn't ever been. Then she shook her head. "I can't believe this stuff."

Arthur got impatient. "So what is it? A tree house or something?"

"It's a little underground room, kind of like a subterranean lair. He said that it used to be a place of worship. We stayed there for, like, two hours. We could hear the deputies stomping over the ground all around us. Then they left, and he suggested that I run up here to look for you."

I glanced at Arthur. I wondered if he was thinking the same thing that I was. "So the helmets are working," I said, "and we need a place for me to lay down while I enter the spiritual realm."

"He collapsed the second that he turned it on," said Arthur.

"Are you okay?" said Julia, taking my hand.

I nodded. "Of course. The helmet helped. But it's weird how going there freezes up your body."

"What was it like?"

"Kind of gray and empty. I expect that I'll learn more as I explore. But now I know that I need to have a place for my body while I'm gone."

We all looked at each other. "Can Cy fit all of us in that subterranean room?"

"He's down there, waiting for us," she replied.

"Then let's go together," I said. "Each of you, grab a helmet. I'm still a little unsteady and need my hands free."

We moved slowly down the slope, attempting to stay behind shrubs and trees as much as possible. I didn't know where the sheriff's deputies were, and I was determined to stay out of their line of sight.

Then we crossed the native graveyard. I flinched as we got there, but we had no trouble setting foot onto the land, or passing through it. Cy had been telling the truth when he said, after the confrontation with Little Horn, that his ancestors had left the place.

"Now where?" asked Arthur.

Julia pointed up the opposite slope. "It's up there, between some bushes. Kind of hidden. It could be a hard climb if you are feeling tired, William."

We passed the ruins and, about five hundred yards later, turned to go up the slope. We cut through the boulders, the rocks, the short grasses, the shrubs, until we reached a level part of the forest. This was part of the reservation I hadn't ever explored. I stopped to rest for a moment, turning to survey the valley, and my heart sank. The ruins of the Hall of Knowledge were below us now. The utter devastation that Roivas had caused was on clear display. There was nothing left. As we traversed the slope, I noticed fresh rocks on the slope. I felt a pang of sadness, remorse and even anger—I'd spent a lot of time in that room, drawing. I'd learned to love it, even if I hadn't totally understood it.

Then Julia pulled on my elbow. "We're just about there. It's between those two small trees, straight ahead. There's a hatch on the ground."

I saw the two trees that she was indicating, and we headed over. They were spaced about twenty feet apart, and on the ground between the slim trunks was indeed a wooden hatch. It was fitted snugly inside a square of stones and blended into the ground.

I leaned down and picked it up by the edge.

When I pulled it away, the worried, creased face of Cy appeared beneath me. He was looking up at us, and he was holding a piece of wood in his hand like a club. As he recognized that it was us, his face softened and his grip on the wood weakened. "William, am I glad to see you again," he said.

"You're going to be even happier when you see what we've got with us," I said.

"What do you have?"

Arthur handed me a helmet, and I passed it down to Cy in the hole. He took the thing and looked at it. "It works?" he asked.

I nodded. "I just went into the spiritual realm with it. Just for a few seconds."

He made a get-in-here motion with his hand. "Hurry, before they see you. I've got something to show you, too."

I went first and lowered myself into the hole. He dragged over a tall step for my feet to land on, and then I went all the way down to the dirt floor. While he helped Arthur and Julia, I looked around.

The underground room was bigger than I'd thought. It was lit by a series of electric torches that had been placed in sconces on the walls around the room. A few chairs were scattered around. A single circle of stones beneath the hatch guarded some blackened embers, which meant that some fires had been made here. The floor and walls were made of hard-packed dirt, but the ceiling was wooden-beam construction, evidently to prevent a collapse. A small shrine against one wall stood empty except for a couple half-melted candles.

Against the other wall stood a long wooden table. It looked handmade and sturdy enough to support a human.

I hoped.

Arthur and Julia had both landed inside by now, and Cy dragged the wooden hatch shut. Instantly the room felt damp, more claustrophobic.

"What do you think?" he said, gesturing to the space. "My people have been seeking refuge here for generations. Mostly from the rain, but they tell me it was used to hide from enemies in the old days."

"We could've used it when Little Horn arrived," said Julia.

"It wouldn't have mattered, not against him."

"I think it's cozy," said Arthur. "What do you think, William?"

I shook my head. "Are you nuts? Anyway, I'm going to lay right there on that table and put on the helmet and enter the spiritual realm."

Cy nodded, in a way that told me he'd always known that this was how things had to go. "Good, but first I have got a few things to show you. Sit. You're going to need all possible knowledge."

CHAPTER NINETEEN

We gathered around the table, and Cy poured a beverage from a box that he'd kept under a tarp in the corner. It was earthy and floral and sweet all at the same time.

"What is this stuff?" said Arthur.

"Earth extract," explained the old native. "My grandmother showed me how to collect twenty-four different types of plants in this valley and how to crush them together. I was making it earlier today when Julia came and told me that the deputies were arriving."

Despite the warming liquid, I shuddered as I thought about the horrible events of the last couple days. "Do you think they've found the deputy's body yet?"

"Definitely," said Cy. "They had dogs. But enough about those matters. We need to talk about the spiritual realm. Right, Julia?"

She nodded, and I realized that there'd been conversations between the two of them that I hadn't been privy to. She reached into a bag and produced drawings from the Hall of Knowledge and spread them out before us. They were dirty and stained and crinkled. I wasn't surprised; after all, I'd crawled handcuffed through the tunnel with them, stood out in the pouring rain with them, been arrested with them, and faced down Roivas with them.

Cy hummed to himself as his eyes scanned the pages. They were packed full of mostly indecipherable symbols. Indecipherable to me, at least. But I still didn't know exactly how to interpret them, not like Cy, so Arthur and Julia and I were more or less bystanders, waiting for the interpretation to be handed to us.

"Look here," he finally began. "The L.E. communicate with symbols because that's how things are done in the spiritual realm. And this is a record of what they're trying to tell us, and it is very serious in tone."

"So you mean there are no jokes?" Arthur asked, in what I guess was an attempt to crack a joke.

Cy shook his head. "It's really not that kind of place."

That shut Arthur up. He'd probably never considered his own mortality before.

"William already knows that I've analyzed the previous patterns in the symbols, the ones that he drew. What I've done is compare those with yours, Julia."

He spread out two columns of papers. The ones on the left were the old ones that I'd drawn. The ones on the right were the new ones that Julia had drawn.

"And I circled all the changes in red."

I leaned forward and saw that on the new column, there were several symbols circled in red, maybe twenty in all. "Some of them were minor changes, to civilizations that had already reached Final Ignition. Remember that the Hall of Knowledge is like a message board. Some of them were just giving updates."

He crossed out many of the symbols with a black pen. "But some weren't in those columns. I found some in *our* civilization's column."

His finger landed on a string of four symbols. All four were circled in red marker. I didn't dare disregard the messages, not after the previous messages had pointed me so squarely to the flash drive buried in the cemetery.

"What are they?" asked Arthur.

"Come look for yourselves."

I crowded over the page with Arthur. Julia stayed nearby but didn't try to see. She must've remembered them, or maybe she was thinking about her father.

The four symbols were a circle of arrows pointing inward, a geodesic ball, and a spiral leading down to a disc.

"That's a fullerene," said Arthur, pointing to the second one. "Sometimes we call them Buckyballs after the guy who discovered them, Buckminster Fuller. Well, some Germans discovered geodesic domes, but he perfected a practical kit. What does this mean?"

I shook my head. "It's impossible to know until you're in the moment. Then you'll know how to use them, if you're lucky."

Cy looked at me. "And it's up to you to notice them, my friend."

I stared hard at the four symbols. The circle of arrows pointing inward, the geodesic ball, the spiral, and the disc.

"I got it," I said.

Julia was standing nearby. I noticed her moody facial expression and touched her arm. "What's the problem?"

She looked at me with hurt in her eyes. "I think those changed," she said.

"What do you mean?"

She pointed at the pages. "I mean, when I first sketched

them, that's what they looked like. But when I looked back a few minutes later, there was a fifth one."

"On that string of symbols?"

"Yes."

"What did it look like?"

She sighed, crossed her arms, thought about it for a while. "I can't really remember."

"Try."

She shut her eyes and concentrated. I could see a vein throbbing on the side of her forehead.

"No, I don't remember."

That left me a little downcast. I nudged the edge of the table leg with my toe, and then shrugged. "Well, I'll just do the best I can."

"I'm sorry," she said, "I really should've added it, but there was so much confusion. And I'm upset, you know?"

"It's okay, Julia. These symbols have already helped so much."

"William, it's time," said Cy.

I lay on the table. The wooden slats were hard under my back, and my shoulder blades were pressing against the hard wood.

"We should put something under you," said Julia.

"Do we have a blanket or a pad or something?" asked Arthur.

Cy grunted. He turned and rummaged through the freestanding closet, then finally turned to a dusty tarp. "Only this. Nobody sleeps here."

I cleared my throat and said, "If you fold that up, it'll be perfect under my upper back."

Julia dutifully folded it into squares, and I sat up while she laid it beneath me. Then I lay back down.

"How's that?"

"Perfect."

Cy came over. "I don't know how long this will take you. But I promise that we will take care of your body while you're here."

I looked at him and the others. "Don't touch the helmet, okay? Don't pull me out. Just take care of my body, give me some water, and I'll come back when I'm ready. Promise?"

Arthur gulped and nodded. Julia did too, her eyes wide with fright.

Then Cy spoke very deliberately. "You should know that there is a chance that you might … stay."

I felt every hair on my body stand on end. That thought had occurred to me too, but I didn't want to bring it up. Stay. It sounded too much like death. Was it death? I realized I didn't even know what "life and death" were anymore.

Arthur cut in. "Wait, wait—if you die in the afterlife, what happens? I mean, is that even *possible*?"

I was reminded of that old wives' tale about having a dream that you're falling, and if you hit the ground in the dream, it means you've died in real life. "I don't know, Arthur."

Cy addressed all of us. "If you're damaged in the spiritual realm, you may be damaged, period. It's possible that your spirit could stay."

"So this could be a one-way trip?" asked Arthur.

"Maybe. I don't know because I haven't been there. Sonny would've known more." He grew sad and stepped away from the table for a moment.

Arthur came over and offered his fist. "Hey, send me a message or something. If you can."

I gave his fist a bump. "I'll try."

"And don't take too long. Get this over with and come back.

We have a life to live." He tried to put on a happy grin, but I could see that he was nervous for me.

I smiled. "Yeah, we do."

Arthur leaned over and gave me a hug. Then he stepped away, and Julia stepped forward. I was feeling as though I were watching my own funeral.

"William, you have to come back," she said. "Like, you're really important—and I'm sorry that I didn't see that before."

"I'm not *that* important."

"Yes, you are. I've seen it. Do your best against Roivas. Don't blink. Don't back down. Just demolish him!

"I will," I assured her, although I was anything but confident.

She bent down and kissed me on the lips. It was a real kiss too, lingering, open-mouthed, not one of those peck-and-run type of kisses. I could feel her passion entering my body. I gave her a half-hearted smile.

Then Cy stepped up, his thick, leathery hand outstretched. "I only had an idea of what might happen when I picked you up on the road that day. But I'm glad I did. I'm proud that we've helped each other in this fight. I'm proud to call you friend. And I'm proud to help you along whatever path the universe intends for you."

"Same here," I croaked. It was exceptionally hard to hear him saying goodbye to me. How could someone mean so much to me in such a short time? I realized it had to do not only with who I was now, but what I'd learned about the human condition.

"I'll try to contact all of you," I said.

Arthur stepped forward with the helmet and placed it on my head. It fit snugly.

"Ready?" he said.

"Yep."

His hand arrived at the side of my helmet. "Three, two…"

"One," I said.

I felt him press the button, and that strange sound entered the helmet. The room disappeared, and I knew that I was hurtling toward the biggest challenge of my life.

CHAPTER TWENTY

In an instant, I find myself back in the gray field, the spiritual realm. I lift my hand to try and see it, to find if it is the same as the first time, when it was as though my hands weren't there. They don't seem to be. I look down and around and can't see anything of my own body. There is nothing here except gray sludge that permeates everything. And above my eyes, the two blue lights of the helmet blink intermittently.

Then I hear a strange thrumming.

Whum, whum, whum, whum, whum…

It is distant but strong, and I make my way toward it. The urge to move faster possesses me, but it feels as though I am encased in soft clay, or in an early video game with poor sensitivity to directed action.

I move in the direction of the sound, ordering my nonexistent legs to *move*. It grows more insistent. *Whum, whum, whum, whum, whum…*

Then, I see a vague greenish light coalescing ahead. I've seen that before; it is the same light that gathered on the ceiling of the Hall of Knowledge, kind of. It is diffused and curling and eerie, but it isn't off-putting. It draws me in.

I move beneath it and peer up. It seems to peer back at me, and then a tendril of green light snakes out and encircles my head, or at least where my head used to be. I can feel its strange presence.

You are William who changes things.

I change things?

You're a Change Agent.

Yes, I am.

The green smoke drifts away into the gray sludge, and soon I am alone again. It is a strange encounter. The smoke didn't seem to tell me anything new, or to interact. It just wanted to verify my identity, but surely it knows who I am.

I don't stay alone for long—there is movement around me. Out of the corner of my eye, I spot strange dark lumps, forming and coming toward me, like an animal moving under a blanket. They are now around me, and I can see protuberances forming, what seems to be heads, limbs, even tails. It is grotesque—yet I can't look away.

One of the strange shapes draws alongside me. Immediately I feel a strong desire to injure, to damage something, anything. I don't recognize these feelings. These *aren't* my feelings. I am not normally an angry guy.

Then I realize that these feelings aren't coming from me— they are from this misshapen lump. Suddenly, it begins stretching and moving, as though something inside is pushing against its elastic sides, trying to escape.

I do not want to find out what it is so I turn away. Behind me, the lumps make a low screech, an orchestra of dissonant harmonies, horribly distorted. I ignore them and continue to move on.

I move along for a while. I don't know how long. It is impossible to tell how much time elapsed here in the spirit realm, or if there even *is* time. I don't have to expend any energy, and I never get hungry or thirsty. There is only the endless gray sludge.

Then I remember one of the symbols that Cy showed me. It was the circle of arrows pointing inward. I stop my progression and think about that. I have been moving forever, it seems, but making no progress. Maybe that symbol is supposed to represent me.

So I turn myself inward. I concentrate on my own life, on my own travels, on my own people. My mother immediately comes into my presence. Her image is unclear; nowhere near as sharp as Grace's face was, which tells me that she isn't as advanced as Grace. Maybe she isn't as advanced as I am either, or maybe she just hasn't been in the spiritual realm long enough to learn how to navigate it. But I can still tell that it is her.

Mom, I say.

William.

I'm sorry.

It's okay. I'm happy here. There is no reason to grieve.

You know I'm not dead, Mom. Or whatever dead was to us there.

We know, honey.

The way she says that last line makes me realize that I'm standing out here like someone barging into a formal party wearing an outrageous costume. The helmets are ingenious, but they are just an imitation, a shallow shortcut to the experience that has been the greatest mystery of human existence. Those who had truly crossed knew things that even I, a Change Agent, could only hope to understand.

I have to fight Roivas, I say.

Roivas isn't something you want to fight.

But he killed you. If I don't confront him, he'll kill me, too.

Everyone has to enter the spiritual realm.

This stops me in my tracks. Is she implying that the forces of evil are too strong, and that I shouldn't stand up to them? This strikes me as absurd, and I think about all those people throughout history who suffered under evil, and the others who stood up to evil. It seems to me that evil is a never-ending thing, and fighting it should be a never-ending task. And I can't let go of the idea that murdering human beings is evil, that killing in the manner of the Samurai is just a way of sending someone to another life.

It hurts me to do it, but I turn away from my mother. I can feel her presence disappear behind me.

I must complete this journey on my own.

I struggle with where to turn next, but I remember the second symbol that Cy had showed us. It was a geodesic ball, what Arthur called a fullerene. I remember hearing our chemistry teacher talk about that the previous year. A fullerene is a molecule of carbon, and it is found on earth and in outer space. Material science was starting to make good use of that structure, I was told.

I wonder if that will help me find Roivas.

I look deep inside myself and think hard, concentrating on that shape. Gradually, as I focus, the gray sludge disappears, and I find myself inside a shining prism. I look around, in every direction. It is a series of pentagonal and hexagonal interlocking rings. There are ten in total, and as I watch, seven of the ten light up. After having been suspended in sludge for however long, I find this beautiful and exhilarating.

I am suspended in the middle of the spherical prism, and as I try to move toward the outer edges, the prism moves away from me. I try again, in the opposite direction, but the prism moves the other way. I feel like a hamster in a clear ball. I can run in any direction but never escape.

Then, a brilliant, beautiful light approaches the prism from the outside. I can feel it watching me. It circles the prism, faster and faster, such that I feel like I am in the middle of the centrifuge, or on that Death Spiral ride at the amusement park, where the floor falls out from under you as you are pinned against the wall. It is nothing but a blur of light and speed, and it speaks to me—a single word.

Go!

At that second, I am filled with an incredible sense of love. My entire being is overwhelmed with a sense of unity, of belonging. Suddenly, I know that everything in the world and beyond is connected by a series of cosmic strings, much like a spider web, and if you pluck one string, the entire universe vibrates.

The light disappears, the prism falls away from me, and I am now standing at the edge of a deep canyon, a black hole with a single path leading into it. I hadn't thought of this place. The light must've put me here. I can still feel it inside of me. I am going to carry it everywhere.

As I begin to descend, I can't help thinking that I just looked into the face of God, or the Ancient Engineer. That term sounds so familiar to me—what is it?

I circle down into the darkness. It is like a spiral staircase, except that there are no steps, and I have no legs. But there is an undeniable spiral descent, and as the gray turns to black, the spiritual realm soon begins to take on an undeniably darker feel.

Soon I see a series of small beings scuffling in the mud. They look like small pieces of waste, and I sense from them an endless array of uncontrollable urges. The small creatures tussle with one another, biting, snapping. Their voices sound like small, vicious animals. It almost feels like they have been wound up like a child's toy.

I move lightly through them, barely looking down. They say don't argue with idiots, because idiots always drag you down to their level. If I try to interact with any of these blunted spirits, they will do exactly that. Besides, they aren't who I need to confront.

I need to confront Roivas.

The path carries me farther down into the darkness, and the snuffling animal sounds of the creatures thankfully disappear behind me. The path is murkier, and I can rely only on my intuition to guide me farther.

A putrid, icy rain begins to fall, and I'm now standing in a field of slush. It smells terrible. I can hear a commotion on the near horizon. I move over to it and see a group of spirits rolling in the vile, wet earth, as if they are bound to the ground, trapped. They are howling and are just as blunted as the other group, no facial features or even recognizable body parts, but they are somehow larger, almost like a herd of walrus. I also sense from them that they once had voracious appetites—full of food, drink, drugs, gambling, everything, until nothing was enough to satisfy their urges.

Even worse, standing in the middle of this group is a guardian—a three-headed dog. It barks at the victims and mauls them with its claws, and they scream in horror as its sharp talons rakes them. I shudder as I imagine being stuck in such an existence.

Suddenly, one of the dog's heads turns and catches sight of me. Its nostrils flare, and its ears shoot back as it bares its teeth. Then the other two heads turn, and as the beast rotates its torso to face me, I know that I have to think of something to defend myself. I instinctively reach down and scoop a handful of the putrid mud and quickly shove it into the dog's nearest mouth. I don't know why I chose to do that, but it works. The dog head chews on the horrible stuff. Then I pick up two more handfuls and shove them in the other two mouths.

This distracts the dog heads enough to let me slide by. Soon the beast falls into the darkness behind me as well.

My journey continues, and time no longer holds any meaning to me. I can't even think about anybody from back home, or what they might be doing. I am living in the present to an extent that I have never done before.

But soon I sense that I am no longer alone. To my left side I notice a spirit with a sprightly hue is bouncing along, almost as though I invited him to join me on my journey. It's attractive, but I feel something else at the same time.

William, it says.

You know my name.

Help me, and I'll help you.

Tell me about this proposal.

I'll give you power in this realm if you give me Arthur.

I feel alarmed. *So you know Arthur?*

Yes, and we want him.

There is nothing more to be said. Anybody who asks me to turn over my friends for personal gain is clearly the enemy. Even as I continue moving, I hear the spirit's lizard-like babbling following me until it too finally fades into the darkness.

I hear the ringing of steel upon steel, and the shouts of men. This is mixed with crying, and I can physically feel the agony of the hurt. Something rolls past, and I realize it is the image of a human head. I see something taking shape in the darkness in front of me—the outline of a mushroom cloud.

I know where I am.

I must have entered the part of the spiritual realm that belongs to the most violent. I can feel the rude animal anger everywhere, smell the death, taste the bitter iron of blood in my mouth. It is shocking to feel the sensory input again after so much time here in the spiritual realm.

Soon I am passing through a battlefield. The shapes around me are indistinct, but I feel that they condemned themselves in the afterlife to more of what they'd done on the earthly realm.

Something jars me from behind, and I whirl around. A red skull with orange flaming eye sockets attacks me. It fervently tries to dominate and subjugate me. I suddenly feel that its very essence is the epitome of violence. What kind of person must this spirit have been?

I decide to traverse the battlefield, leaving the angry spirit in my wake, dodging the bursts of viciousness that explode like bombs all around me. Finally, it all falls away behind me, and the path appears again. I follow it and descend into space once more.

This time, the path is steeper and darker than ever before. I continue for what seems like an eternity, but soon the path peters out completely.

It isn't even gray sludge. Rather, it is complete blackness, total lack of all sensory input. I feel like I'm sealed in my own tomb.

Then a small flicker of light, like a flame, comes at me. I am entranced as it draws closer; it is being cupped in the hands of someone who looks recognizably human.

As he draws closer, I draw in a breath.

It is Sonny.

✧✧✧

He looks the same as I remember, with his stooped posture and wrinkled face. I know that he is presenting himself to me the way that I know him. This is the way things go here.

Sonny draws up close, lifts his face, and offers a crinkled smile. For a moment, I think I see something different in his face, something in the way he is looking at me. But I dismiss it.

You're lost, William.

I'm looking for Roivas.

Roivas isn't looking for you.

Roivas killed my family, killed you, and wants to kill me.

His face grows darker. *I can lead you to Roivas.*

I follow him. As we travel down the path, a virtual house of horrors flocks around us—odd creatures with several heads shrieking, elongated shadows. I stay as close as possible to Sonny's light. This is the one thing I can depend on.

The path becomes a spiral ramp that grows steeper and steeper. Sonny slides down the path, and I follow. Soon we are slipping, falling, tumbling, careening down the path—until we land on what looks like a wide disc. A galaxy of stars surrounds us. I am surprised at how physical the spiritual realm is, given that we don't have bodies.

Where have you brought me, I ask.

To Roivas.

I open myself up, trying to sense where the malevolent Roivas might be, but nothing of its presence comes through. I just stand there on the disc, surrounded by the galaxy.

Then I notice Sonny looking at me. The light in his cupped hands begins to turn a sickly green. His features are changing.

Sonny?

I watch as the face disappears and becomes as smooth as the shiny surface of an eggshell. Then it darkens into a mass, and from that mass emerges a face. I recognize this face! From deep within this creature an energy is gathering, and when the navy-blue pinstripe suit and shiny shoes begin to materialize, I realize that I have made an awful mistake.

This isn't Sonny. Of course it isn't.

This is Roivas.

CHAPTER TWENTY-ONE

I step back to the edge of the disc. This is as far as I can physically get from Roivas. An intense fear fills me—the same fear I felt when I faced this creature outside the Hall of Knowledge, and again in the graveyard.

"You betrayed me," I say.

"I'm evil. What did you expect?"

This takes me by surprise. It is a stark acknowledgment of the very fact of its existence.

"You killed my parents. You tried to kill Grace. You want to kill me."

"And yet you have hunted for me."

"Our civilization is trying to achieve Final Ignition—and you're standing in our way."

I can see the horns that are beginning to sprout through the cloth of its navy-blue pinstripe suit. It sends icy chills that travel into my very soul. The horns grow, one inch, two inches, three. It is horrifying, and I can feel the sadistic glee that he derives from seeing my terror.

"Little Horn," I say. "They call you by many names."

His head tilts.

"The names change but I will always remain. You can't kill me. You can't stop me. You can only become one with me. Join me, William. You and I are the same. Touch me."

Outrage grows in my soul, the same feeling I felt outside the Hall of Knowledge. It gathers itself from the toes of my feet to the top of my scalp, and then it starts to explode out of me.

I deliver the strongest display of psychic force, whatever my new power is, that I had ever used—and I aim it directly at this unholy creature in front of me. I watch the force emanate from my being and zip toward him. Whereas Julia's cousin had been blown backward by such a display, Roivas barely moves. It glances off him like a pebble bouncing off an enormous rock monolith.

He stands there, grinning wickedly.

I slump. There is no doubt that I failed. The only question is how badly had I failed, and whether I will survive. Will I exist here? Like these tormented sprits? Will I be with my parents, in what is clearly a better place?

"You wait," he says.

"For what?"

No answer. To my surprise, Roivas disappears. The only thing remaining is his horrible grin hanging in space, and then finally this vanishes, too.

I find myself alone on the disc. I turn around and go back to the path that we used to tumble down here… but it is gone. I peer up at the galaxy. That has disappeared, too. Then I look down, and the disc has disappeared beneath me. I try to move, but I feel as if I am encased in frozen plastic. It is impossible.

I am suspended in nothingness.

✧✧✧

As I wait, and what must have been "time" rolls by, I realize I am in a prison, one without walls. It is a prison of sensory deprivation, which is a peculiar type of torture, one that on earth drives people to madness.

All I can do is think.

There is nothing else—nothing to see, nothing to feel, nothing to explore. Even the blue lights in the helmet above my eyes are barely blinking, just enough to remind me that I am, in fact, still alive, in my human form, somewhere.

I know that Roivas has done something awful to me, has ensnared me in a web of his own making. Now there is nothing I can do to get out. It gives me time to reflect, but there isn't much to reflect on, and it makes me turn madly inward. Roivas assumed the form of Sonny, and I stupidly followed him down into this weird corner of the spiritual realm. And now I am paying for it. If I am truly passed over, then he will keep me for all eternity.

But I have not crossed over, not yet. I am still alive, somewhere in the living earthly realm. The helmet lights told me so.

The problem is that I don't have any options. I don't know how to navigate this place well enough to get out of my predicament. I have to simply wait and see what happens next. I am a fly caught in a spider's silky web. And there I hang, frozen in nothingness. It feels like years. I replay in my head everything that has happened in my life—my First Ignition, my early childhood memories. If you're denied all sensory input, your brain ultimately unlocks all your memories, ones that you didn't even know you have the keys to retrieve. Eventually I even remember the moment of my birth.

After what feels like an eternity, I feel something approaching.

It is an old man cupping a candle. I see again that it must be Roivas masquerading as Sonny, and I feel the outrage gathering inside me. Following close behind is a shape I don't recognize. It is spherical and has two small blinking lights.

As they draw closer to me, I recognize the form and draw in my breath. That spherical shape is the other helmet. A moment later, it arrives, and I can see the face that is beneath it.

It is Cy. Roivas has used the image of Sonny on Cy, just as he did to me.

I watch as Cy and Roivas drop onto the same disc that I'd found myself on. Then I see Cy gesture to Sonny——and the old man transforms into Roivas again. It is the same transformation that occurred with me earlier. The navy-blue pinstripe suit, shiny shoes, smooth egghead that morphs into the face with the unnatural grin. I try to scream, but I can't make a sound. I can't even reach out with my soul. Whatever Roivas has encased me in is enough to block my entire existence. I watch Cy. I can sense his fear, his anger. They exchange some words that I'm not allowed to hear. Then Cy tries to reach out to the evil creature—but Roivas slashes him with his horned arm, the same way he'd slashed Sheriff Winters. I see Cy stagger backward. The blue lights on his helmet blink, weaker now. Roivas grins lewdly at me, and then makes a motion. The plastic encasing falls away. I immediately rush toward him, but as I approach the disc, Roivas sees me coming and disappears again. That horrible grin hangs in the air for one final second, then disappears too. Why hasn't he done the same to me? What is he waiting for?

I arrive at my elderly friend. Without a body, he hasn't bled out, but I sense that his life force has grown weaker.

"Cy, why did you come?" I say.

"We didn't know what was happening. You didn't send us any signs."

"Roivas tricked both of us, and now we can't get out."

Cy just sits there, not saying anything. He looks around at the galaxy, at the disc beneath his feet.

"This is the place that my ancestors described. They told a story about a round plate that held souls of our people."

"How did the story end?"

"When the people learned selflessness."

I look directly at him. I don't know what he means. How do you learn selflessness in a place without any other people? I have been trapped inside myself for what seems like forever.

Then I realize maybe *that* has been the problem. Maybe I've been too wrapped up in myself to notice anything else, and that Roivas hasn't, in fact, imprisoned me. Maybe I imprisoned myself. After all, I broke out of that state only after I'd seen an injustice being done to Cy.

We stay there on the disc, each of us thinking about the next steps we can take. I know that Cy is growing significantly weaker because of his wounds. It is as though his life energy is leaking out of him. His comments are growing progressively muddier, more confused.

I realize that this is a glimpse into the mind of a person who is dying. It is ironic to be dying in the spiritual realm, but I can't explain it any other way. He is simply less of a presence.

"Don't go, Cy," I say. "Stay here and be strong."

"I'm trying."

We both sense movement and as we turn our heads we see a very familiar sight.

Sonny is coming down the path, cupping a candle in his hands. Roivas again. A woman is trailing behind the evil creature, and I don't have to see the image of the face that she is projecting to know who she is, because the strength of her presence can't be mistaken for anybody else.

Grace presents herself the way that I had seen her the first time I checked into the spiritual realm, just for those few seconds—just her face, purely feminine, soft, the way that I knew it back home.

Grace sees me and Cy, and her face lights up. "William, you found Sonny too."

"I was sending a warning. Grace—"

Then, Roivas sends a powerful ball of anger shooting toward me. I watch my message get encased in the ball and then swallowed into darkness. Grace will never receive it, because I'm muzzled. Cy tries to express the same, but Roivas sends another ball barreling toward him.

Then Sonny makes a motion, and I feel myself encased in the same weird plastic. I look over and see that Cy is encased just like me. We are just hanging there, as though frozen in ancient sap that has turned to amber, all because we represent something.

The truth.

Grace doesn't know to whom she is talking. I feel myself growing more agitated. It is as horrific as watching a friend walk into a buzz saw.

Roivas reveals himself to her—the navy-blue pinstripe suit, shiny shoes, smooth egghead that morphs into the face with the unnatural grin. Once again, I try to scream, but once again I can't make myself heard or known.

But I can see Grace's face as the transformation occurs. I can see the horns sprouting through the suit. And I see the look of horror on her face as she realizes that, even here in the spiritual realm, her brother still has her by the throat.

Then their communication comes in loud and clear, as though I have been let into a private conference call. Presumably Roivas doesn't see me as a threat anymore, not since he encased me in this special insulation.

"What are you doing to my friends?" she asks.

"You've changed," says Roivas. I notice that he ignored the question.

"I'm the same."

"So am I, Grace. I have been the same for all eternity. You knew me as child in the last iteration."

"But you are part of me, Grace. We were twins. We share the same DNA. When you denounce me, you denounce yourself. These two came here to defeat me—your own brother. You can't let them."

His face grows sad, in a mockery of sensitivity. I hold my breath, expecting Grace's answer. It doesn't come. I expect a forceful denunciation of Roivas, instead there is only silence. I look at her. She's wavering. She can't see his deception.

I turn to Cy.

"We have to help her."

"No. She has free will. Let her make her own decision."

This doesn't make any sense to me. If she is making the wrong decision, then she needs help. But Cy's comment is interesting. What if this entire earthly world is a trial run to see how humans handle the question of free will?

I look back at her. She looks at me, and then at Cy. Then she looks back to Roivas.

"I don't know, Roland."

Roivas's face twitches. It is either from hearing the birth name or from the strain of pretending to look sympathetic. Then his facial features disappear into a dark jumble of anger, and I remember what happened the last time I saw that.

"You are not to stand in my way. You are on my side."

"Roland, I don't know."

I watch Roivas raise the horrible horned arm and bring it across Grace's side. She emits a sound of great pain that pierces my soul. I find a flood of compassion rushing through me, mixed with an intense need for justice, but that plastic casing keeps me in place.

"You have Proof. Use it," urges Cy.

I know what he means. I concentrate everything that I have upon breaking out of this strange spiritual prison that Roivas has put me in, twice. I dive into the deepest well of strength and compassion and scoop it up and hurl it with all my might—

And to my surprise, the plastic casing falls away.

I understand why it fell away. I did not break that casing with anger. Roivas knew how to defend against that. I broke out because the anger was mixed with compassion for someone being hurt.

Selflessness.

That was all it took. Roivas doesn't understand selflessness or charity. It is the chink in its terrible horned armor—the act of caring for another person.

Free from the cage, I swoop over to Roivas. The horrific spine turns to me, the hundreds of sprouted horns creating a garish décor on its back that looks a lot like a bed of nails. I gather up the same sensation as when gritting my teeth and bear down hard and find another enormous wellspring of energy and strength…and hurl it directly at the monster's back.

This time, with Roivas caught off guard, it makes an impact. Roivas staggers, and I can sense that the creature is off balance, maybe even weakened. Then Roivas finds his footing again and turns to me.

I shrink back. His eye sockets are totally empty.

I would be frightened if there were flames leaping out, or vampire bats, or anything, really. But to see pure emptiness in someone's eyes is the most frightening thing of all. It means that there is absolutely no regard for another life. It is like staring into the eyes of a dead snake. There is no there *there*.

"Die," he says.

"You can't kill me. I'm already in the spiritual realm."

"I can make sure you never return to earth."

"You can't kill me."

And then he changes tack: "I can give you what you want!"

"What do I want?"

"I know your thoughts, William. Girls, money, adventure. I can give you all of these. Just ask."

He knows. He knows my weaknesses, my lusts and desires. I had been a shallow, self-absorbed little nobody, and he knows it. But I'm changed.

"You can't give me what I want now."

Then he screams and I watch Roivas lift that horned arm. A moment later I feel the full power of the nearly demonic presence upon me. It is a rending sensation, my clothing, skin, my soul itself tearing apart. I realize that Roivas is slashing me, over and over.

I fall back, back, back—and Roivas keeps coming, coming, coming. His arm slashes me, over and over. If I weren't already in the spiritual realm, I would prepare for death. The blue lights above my eyes on the helmet are almost totally dead.

"Die," Roivas says again.

The arm goes up for a final time. I brace for it, knowing that it won't be long before my life is finished. I will spend all eternity here, slave to this horrible entity, Little Horn, the embodiment of pure evil.

"Stop," Grace says.

Roivas pauses, begins to turn. Before his movement can be completed, a massive burst of energy lights up the entire disc. An unearthly screech emits from Roivas's mouth, a cacophony of pain, a voice carrying the agony of hundreds of centuries of death and destruction.

Grace. I realize that Grace has tapped into Proof, the same empathy, the same longing for justice that I felt. And I feel relieved. She has snapped out of Roivas's gaslighting and directed all of the considerable power upon her own brother.

I look over at Cy. He's still suspended in the plastic casing—but as I watch, it dissolves around him, enough for him to break out. Of course, I don't know how those force fields were formed, not exactly, but I suspect that they depend upon the strength of the host.

This means that Roivas is weakened.

I see another opportunity to fight this demon of an entity. I look deep within myself for more rage, more anger, but I come up empty. I have very little of that left. I realize that those feelings are the opposite of what selfishness represents. Then it hits me: Grace is not feeding the hate and anger and the rage. That is Proof where the power is coming from. I know now that I must have compassion. There's no way I can love something like Roivas. But I can choose not to hate him. Then the answer rains down on me like bricks falling from the sky. Hate from others is his fuel. Remove the fuel, diminish the flame. This might be the most dangerous thing of all for

Roivas, and I tap into that, and then I speak to him of things I know he can't understand or tolerate.

"I won't hate you anymore," I say. And with that the fire that is raging inside Roivas diminishes a bit. It is like an out-of-control campfire that's just receiving its first splash of water.

Roivas looks at me with that dark mass of smudged facial features. I sense that he is confused, so I double down on my intent.

"I won't hate you anymore. And you don't have to hate either."

I don't know if it will work. Still, my intent is direct, and I know that he sees that my heart is true. He tries to shrink away, but Grace steps up.

"I don't hate you, Roland. Let us show you how to stop hating."

"We can show you," I add.

Cy comes alongside us. "There's always time to change. I won't hate you anymore, Little Horn. Stop hating. Save yourself."

Roivas' face configures and reconfigures itself into a hundred different faces. I see an ancient Roman executioner, a blood-soaked Viking warrior, a Mongol horseman, a Mayan chief, a Nazi soldier. These and many others flash across the visage with startling rapidity. I realize that Roivas has been all of these people, and has created chaos and destruction in all these times and places. Roivas is the embodiment of the very impulse that prevents humanity from reaching Final Ignition.

"*No!*" thunders Roivas.

And then Roivas vanishes right before our eyes, no grin hanging in the air this time.

Only silence.

CHAPTER TWENTY-TWO

W hat seemed like an instant later, I realized I had arrived back in my human body.

Everything was dark, and then I sensed that it was because I couldn't open my eyes, no matter how hard I tried. So I wiggled the fingers of my left hand. I could feel them clenching and unclenching.

"He's moving," a voice says.

I felt hands on my body, and my head being lifted, and the helmet being slipped off, and then my head being set down.

"William, come back to us," said the voice. I realized that it belonged to Julia.

The hands went all over my body, touching, stroking, massaging. It felt good—a welcome back to the world of nerve endings.

At last I was able to peel open my eyes slightly. I saw Julia and Arthur looking down at me.

"He's back!" said Arthur.

"How are you feeling?" said Julia.

I tried to open my mouth to speak, but it wouldn't move.

Slowly, and with effort, I managed to make a sound like *blarrrgh.*

"Dude, I don't speak helmet," said Arthur. "Can you translate?" he guffawed.

I wanted to punch him out of happiness, but I couldn't move my arms. It was so good to hear his smart-aleck comments again.

Soon I was able to move my head. I saw that I was still on the table in the underground room. My friends had apparently kept a watch by my body.

"You were gone for a long time," said Julia.

Arthur was massaging my feet, which was pretty generous of him, when you think about it. "Three whole days!"

My eyes got wide, and I looked at the two of them. "Only three days?"

"Hey, look, his tongue is working again," said Arthur. "Hey, say it again! Say *blarrrgh.* "

Julia glared at him, handing me a cup of water. "We thought we might have to carry you up to the cabin if you were going to be gone any longer."

I took a drink, found my voice again. "Seriously, it feels like I've been gone a hundred years. No joke."

Arthur shrugged. "Nope, just three days. We've been right here. I was teaching Julia how to play poker right next to your head." He flashed a deck of cards to illustrate.

I said, "And Grace. She was there!"

"We've been worried about her," said Julia.

"No, don't. She is okay. And I know she will speak to me soon, and we'll find her." Then I thought of someone else. Alarmed, I looked around the room. "Where's Cy?"

"Cy left earlier today to look for some food," said Julia.

Now I shot up to a sitting position. "Whoa, whoa, whoa, easy now," said Arthur.

"He didn't look for food, you guys. He came to the spiritual realm. We fought Roivas together."

The two of them looked around. "He took the other helmet when we went out," said Julia. Then her eyes widened. "Hey, I get it! He was with you!"

"We have to find Cy!" Arthur said with genuine concern.

Julia sniffed the air. "There's a storm coming." She looked at Arthur. "We can't just let him sit outside in the rain."

Meanwhile, I was regaining movement in my arms. "Where would he have gone to protect his body while he was in the spiritual realm?"

Julia looked at us. "The graveyard. No doubt."

"Let's go," said Arthur.

I tried to stand up but felt my legs start to give way beneath me. Julia went to grab me, but I caught myself on the edge of the table.

"I'm coming too," I said. "I think."

They had to help me climb out of the underground room. It was late afternoon, and the sky was turning a purplish gray. You could smell something big, weather-wise, on the horizon. Arthur put an arm around me as we went down the long slope back to the graveyard at the center of the valley. On the way, I explained everything that had happened in the spiritual realm.

He didn't say anything for the longest time. "That's the world's best drug trip."

"No drugs," I said. "It's all real. It's on the other side. Roivas is still powerful, but with a much lesser advantage."

"What are you saying?"

"I'm saying that I'd like to go back to confront Roivas again,

but next time, with understanding. Of him, of human selflessness and human graciousness and Proof that love overcomes
hate."

"I don't know," said Julia. "You were lucky to get away from
that once."

By the time we reached the graveyard, I was able to walk
on my own, though a bit unsteadily. I followed Julia and
Arthur as they meandered their way through the sacred
space.

"I see him," said Julia. "There. The blue."

I followed her hand and saw the blue helmet beneath a bush.
We ran over to the location. Sure enough, it was Cy, his fists
rolling and unrolling. He was moaning to himself.

For the next few minutes, I watched as they removed the
helmet, sat him against a tree, massaged his body, and gave him
water. Eventually his eyes opened and found me. He spoke in
a raspy voice. "We almost had Little Horn."

I sighed. "There were three of us, and we still couldn't change him."

"That doesn't mean it can't happen."

Arthur said, "Why didn't you tell us you were going to use
the helmet? We would've laid you next to William."

Cy shook his head. "It's better that we were far apart. I
wanted it to be a sacred journey. For my people." His finger
made a small circle in the graveyard.

Julia was looking at the crowd with a questioning air. "The
only other question—where is Grace?"

"No clue," I said. "But she will come to me."

Cy nodded. "Let's get back to the cabin now."

Cy struggled to get up, so the others helped him get to his
feet. He was shakier than I was, and as we climbed the slope,
Arthur had to carry the elderly Indian on his back.

"You're killing me, Cy," he said, gasping.

"I've been to the afterlife, and it's not so bad," Cy deadpanned in response.

After much struggle, we arrived at the top of the valley, then moved quietly through the pines, so as to approach Cy's cabin the back way. As we drew closer, I held up my hand for the group to stop. We hunkered down in the shadows of the trees and listened.

I heard the low murmur of men's voices from the front of the cabin.

"Someone's there," I whispered.

Julia and I quietly slunk through the trees until we caught sight of the men. They were on Cy's porch, smoking cigars.

It was Sheriff Winters and two deputies. My eyes almost bugged out of my head. He looked perfectly fine and was even laughing at a joke that one of the men had just told.

"Dad!" shouted Julia, leaping up from next to me.

"Stop, no!" I said, but it was too late. The three police officers heard her, whirled around, and drew their weapons. Julia was running across the pine needles to her father.

"Oh, brother," I said, then turned and ran through the shadows back to Cy and Arthur.

It wasn't happening. My legs were like pipes filled with concrete. I hadn't taken five steps when the deputies were on me, slamming me to the ground, my hands pinned behind me.

"It's the runaway killer, boss," said one of them.

The other walked ahead of me a few paces. "We got two more over here. The other kid and the old man."

The deputy turned me toward Sheriff Winters. He was sauntering toward me.

"At last, Mister William Hawk. At last."

I lifted my face to his, trying to contain my hundreds of conflicting emotions. "How did you survive, Sheriff?"

"Survive what?" he said, but his expression told me that he knew.

"The mauling."

The deputy looked at me quizzically. "What mauling?"

"Roivas mauled the sheriff. I saw it happen. A man nine feet tall, covered in horns, slashed him right across the chest."

"Who-vias? You been smoking crack, son?"

By now Cy and Arthur had given up and were being dragged over to the group by the other deputy.

"More lies?" he asked, his arm around Julia. "The prosecutor's going to have a field day with you, son."

But I was determined to find out for myself. "Would you mind opening your shirt, sir?"

The sheriff's eyes went wide and confused. "You want me to open my *shirt*? You turn gay on us, too?"

Idiot, I thought, but I said, "I want to see the injury on your chest."

Grinning egotistically, the sheriff said, "It's been a long time since anyone asked me to flash the six pack, but what the heck."

He unbuttoned the snaps of his uniform and lifted his T-shirt. My eyes couldn't believe what they were seeing, or weren't seeing. His chest was completely normal, no injuries, no scars. But I'd seen him get horribly injured just four days earlier.

Suddenly I knew that the sheriff was part of the mystery, part of the other worlds I was learning about, and that my part in solving it would just continue to deepen. Why hadn't he shown me who he was? Was he tied to Roivas?

"Who are you really?" I said, well aware that I'd get no answer.

His eyes grew serious, and I thought I detected a flash of green in them. "I was about to ask you the same thing. Who *are* you, William?"

"I'm the one who's going to save humanity," I said. Then I nodded to Arthur and Cy, "With their help."

The deputies laughed at that, but the sheriff didn't. I knew I'd hit upon something with him, but it wasn't clear exactly what.

"Come on, let's take you back to the city," he said. "We've got a lot of questions for you."

I was still thinking about him as they loaded the four of us into two different county-sheriff vehicles. Then, as the deputies started the vehicles, I looked out the window at the valley, wondering where Grace could be—and wished her luck.

We were both going to need it.